Waking Up Dead

By K.A. Masterson

ISBN: 9798354399574

Cover design by: Adrian Pasarin
Printed in the United States of America

This book is dedicated to the great J.S. Lawliss for being my first beta reader, editor, proofreader, and writer best friend. Thank you for loving my stories and characters and always encouraging me.

Chapter 1: Saving the Assassin (Suri)

The first time I animated a corpse, I was four years old.

Mama freaked out while Nana laughed so hard she had to wipe tears from her dancing eyes and had to put her fake teeth back into her mouth. Aislynn had died of mushroom poisoning the night before because she chased a mouse into the nearby field and ate mushroom appetizers instead. Except Aislynn purred happily against my leg.

Mama explained that death was a sacred part of living, even for pet cats. When I reanimated the dead, tendrils of life would slip from my soul into the corpse. The more I gave of my soul, the more danger I was in breaking the delicate balance of nature.

Nana's explanation was more amusing. She said I was the most powerful Animator since her great-great-great-great grandmother Suriya Rovana, a well-known Romanian gypsy who'd raised armies for the Turks.

"*My* name is Suriya Rovana!" I exclaimed with excitement, clapping my plump little hands while Mama groaned.

"I knew I shouldn't have given her that name at birth," she'd mumbled, and Nana laughed with pride and foreknowledge. I had no idea what the fuss was about, but Nana was happy instead of fighting with Mama, and Aislynn would be sleeping in my bed again.

The last time I animated a corpse was two hours ago.

A man had been killed rescuing me from two Gargoyles that tried to attack me. Except, too late did I realize my savior isn't exactly a man, and now I'm stuck with a sexy-as-sin Vampire unconscious on my living room area rug.

Aislynn purrs against the new Risen's pant leg, surprising me because the tuxedo cat hates everyone, a side-effect of bringing back a little bit of death from the other side.

I've been staring at the Vampire for about two hours, pushing my sleep well into the early morning hours. In the meantime, since it's of no consequence to either of us, I admire his physique because he's seriously sexy! His hair is dark but not black. Maybe dark brown and short, except in the front, which slightly covers his face. A five o'clock shadow matches his hair color and his eyebrows are thick but not gross. Who would've thought Vampires could regenerate facial hair?

His face is all angles and sharp edges around full lips that pout in sleep. His body frame, though, is exactly the Vampire type. Lithe, tall, and muscular, like a swimmer or a quarterback. Vampires, however, are much faster and stronger than both.

I yawn into my fist and stare with glazed eyes. He hasn't woken up, and I'm falling asleep.

It usually takes a corpse two to six hours before rigor mortis sets in, so Rising has to happen in between that time. If it doesn't, the corpse still reanimates, but more dead than alive. A zombie.

Of course, that fact applies to human corpses. I'm not even sure if an already undead Vampire could become an undead Risen.

But I couldn't let a stake through the heart kill him when he'd taken it for me. It would've killed him had I not touched his hand in time with my bare one before the disintegration of his body from ashes. A thin tendril of red smoke escaped from my palm into his hand, and then we transported to my apartment.

Saving him, though, had been an impulse and a hiccup of judgment. I always wear gloves, especially in public! But somewhere in the vast corridors of the university library's archives department, I'd misplaced them when I was reviewing an ancient text on the cult of the dead in Assyria and Babylonia. In touching the manuscript, I gain better insight into the writer and background of the culture. The wrist-length gloves cover my palm, the only access to transferring my essence and reading the past by touch.

If truth be told, by the time the Gargoyles and Vampire showed up, I was already freaking out because I sensed I was being followed, only aggravating my growing apprehension from having lost the gloves. I thought I was going to get robbed by a masked mugger. Not Gargoyles!

Having animated a Vampire corpse could've been avoided if the Gargoyles hadn't been following me. Unfortunately, skin-to-skin contact doesn't just reanimate the dead. I'm also stuck with their thoughts and feelings, which is *exactly* why I wear gloves, even in the summer. A simple touch opens my mind to people's memories, experiences, and emotions.

By touching the Vampire, I was exposed to his vampiric lifestyle in the seconds it took me to release his hand when we landed on my living room floor. I'd burst into heart-wrenching sobs and scurried away from him. There was so much blood, violence, and rage pouring into my mind from him, a sledgehammer wracking my body in sobs.

Kilian Willingham.

456 years old.

The oldest Vampire I've heard of.

No. The second oldest.

His Sire is the oldest.

I wish I could leave him here and disappear, but Nana would have my hide if I abandoned what I created! I'd rather take my chances with the Risen. So I'll wait around for Kilian to wake up as a Risen, explain what happened, and slip out of his life as quickly as he'd come into mine.

Animating, Blinking, and Psychometry are the rarest gifts among Supernaturals. Very few can raise the dead and give them life again, albeit of subservience. There are more Supernaturals who can teleport, or Blink, which requires honing one's skill with concentration until it becomes natural. But a select few can experience others' entire life history with a single touch. Psychometry is so rare and many Supernatural courts either steer clear of Seers or covet them for their own gain. Having all three skills is extremely rare.

I'm in *that* category. If the warlords of the supernatural underworld find out about me, I'll be exploited without choice. Some legitimate Courts would prize me as their most valuable member, or even of their race, while others will use me to gain power over other Courts.

So, I rarely Blink, wear gloves to avoid Psychometry and only use it when I'm alone in the archives, and never ever Animate.

Except the Vampire Kilian.

My breath shudders, and I sigh heavily. The consequences of Raising a Vampire out in the open is swift and dangerous. There's no way those Gargoyles aren't going to tell their Court about the Animating and most definitely about the Blinking!

After crying my eyes out and wishing I could unsee and unfeel Kilian's mucked-up life, I packed everything I could fit into a duffel bag along with any important personal items and crammed my Audi with enough food and water to survive a week on the road, including a tent, pillow, and blankets. I'll be on the run for a short while, driving my way down to the Bayou to find Nana in hopes her juju magic can hide my essence until this all settles down and the Courts have forgotten me. Probably in a couple centuries.

Ugh!

I wish I could Blink to Nana's and not have to snail-travel like regular humans. But every supernatural action leaves an imprint, and the Blink would lead straight to Nana's house. I can't risk putting her in any unnecessary danger. This is also why I must leave my apartment before the Gargoyles come looking for me! Then again, only the strongest Supernaturals can see the imprint.

Still, I will not take the chance with Nana, and I can't dwell on regrets or what-ifs, only prepare for the inevitable.

Kilian twitches, and I jump with a little squeak. Again. I keep forgetting Nana's early lessons about the supernatural world, including each of my gifts. But I learned the neuroscience of Risen from Kyle Hill when I was twelve. Of course, the YouTuber was referring to zombies. Same difference. Hill was interesting and funny-nerdy.

When I was in high school, I cross-checked the info and concluded that Risen are similar to but not exactly like zombies. Apparently, the essence, or soul as Nana still calls it, shared with corpses, jumpstarts their suffocating cells, which, in turn, jumpstart the brain. The brain's electrical currents then try to fire up the corpse to animate it, and the body takes the shock through its highway of nerves.

The whole process takes two to six hours, from essence to cells to the brain to the body. But still, the Risen doesn't wake.

"Ugh," I mutter under my breath for the umpteenth time, jamming the heels of my palms into my eye sockets. I yawn-groan into my fist and renew my self-pitying regretful thoughts.

I should just leave. Let him wake alone and figure it out on his own. He isn't a stranger to the supernatural, so I don't have to transition him into that world. He'll just spend the rest of his life obsessing over finding me.

But I don't think I can live knowing he'll search his eternity searching for me while I avoid him at every turn. Nana would be horrified at my lack of respect for the Risen and my duty-bound honor as his Mistress. I hate the male-dominated and historically oppressive word *mistress*. But breaking traditions is practically impossible in the supernatural world.

I glance at the digital clock on the mantle, telling me it's almost the witching hour. I should stay awake because it's a sign he'll awake soon. At least, that's what I hope for. Nana is more attuned to the spirit world than I am.

I yawn again, not bothering with the fist since it's not like the Risen could see me rudely yawning into the air. I lean against the sofa cushions and close my eyes, trying not to relive my stupidity at having revealed all my gifts in one night for the life of a damn Vampire!

"That's not nice, Suri," I whisper at my stereotyping of an entire race based on this very violent Vampire. They're really not the vilest creatures in the supernatural world, even though they lack a soul, which is the center of all moral decision-making. Or lack thereof. Vampires are capable of emotions and feelings, like love and hate. But they'll always choose instinct over compassion and empathy because they're ruthless, possessive, self-serving, and arrogant.

Damn it, they *are* among the most vile!

I can't believe I brought one home with me! Nana is going to be so mad, which is even scarier than a Risen Vampire!

My body sinks into the couch, nice and cozy, my eyes growing heavy with sleep. I grab the last pair of black wrist-length satin gloves I left behind, and carefully put them on. After working an eight-hour shift until midnight at the university library, categorizing the Mesopotamian section of the archives and artifacts, and leaving my other pair behind, the last thing I need is touching anyone else, supernatural or not!

Working at the library pays the rent *and* pays me in knowledge. Nana always said the key to survival is knowledge, and knowledge leads to the rest. She's definitely not a runner-up for the Dooms-Day Prepper award!

I snuggle deeper into the couch, certain I won't fall asleep because Kilian is going to wake up soon and, when he does, he's going to be really, *really* upset and disoriented. I'm just resting my eyes, settling the sandy grains gathered from a long day's work, and waiting for the Vampire to Animate. Then I'll share my heartfelt gratitude, profuse apologies, and quick farewell.

Not falling asleep, I tell myself as a blanket of darkness wraps around me, holding me in its warmth and comfort.

Not falling asleep…

Chapter 2: The Risen Vampire (Suri)

I'm startled awake when long fingers wrap around my neck and squeeze. Completely black orbs of anger and death glare at me with unbridled hate. The violence in Kilian's memories flash in his eyes, pumping adrenaline into his veins, scaring the hell out of me.

He yanks me off the couch with one hand and lifts me into the air from my throat. My feet dangle over the floor, and I choke, my breath cut off by his fingers.

"Damn you, Necromancer," Kilian hisses with a fury that burns along my skin. "How dare you turn me into a zombie?"

I try to shake my head, explaining that he's not a zombie because he won't start craving living flesh to compensate for his dying one. But I can't breathe, and my periphery is turning shadowy and dark along the sharp edges of unconsciousness. What he doesn't know is that if he kills me, he'll die, too!

I have to speak so he doesn't kill me. He just needs to hear the voice of his Mistress so he doesn't kill her!

"Not... zomb–" I choke out before I lose sight of his angry eyes behind a blackness that threatens to drag me under.

Kilian releases me, and I fall to my knees, wildly heaving for air. Lightheadedness trips me up, and disorients me, but Kilian doesn't give me much time to enjoy the coveted air he'd deprived me of seconds earlier. He grabs me by my hair and yanks me to my feet. I scream at the yanking but panic when his hand wraps around my throat again. I try not to freak out because the Risen instinct will override his Vampire one, my essence binding him to the Risen code of servitude.

At least, that's what I hope.

Before he squeezes again, I blurt, "You're not a zombie. You won't crave human flesh."

"I crave *human* blood," he threatens, his eyes turning bloody-red, the pupil striated and sick-looking instead of a small pinprick the way Vampire eyes turn when they're hungry.

I inhale sharply, panic turning to fear. Not just any fear, though, because I'm already afraid. This is a dark fear, one I've only felt when Nana is angry, and she'd order me to take a long walk around the bayou and not worry about the alligators because she'd already warned them. I've never seen a Vampire's eyes turn red. Kilian's eyes are *not* just red!

He pulls me against him, large, white fangs dropping from his gums, way too close to my neck. His fangs are thick, only slightly smaller than a Werewolf's, and pointy enough to pierce flesh, muscle, and bone on contact.

My heart hammers in my chest, but I order, "You will not feed from my blood without my consent!"

The power of Necromancy hits Kilian with such force that he quickly drops me and growls like a caged animal, confusion furrowing his brow. His fangs draw back into his mandible, the sickly eyes fading into a stunning silvery gray, clouded with uncertainty. He blinks rapidly until they narrow, angry and hungry again.

"What did you do to me, Necromancer?" Kilian demands in a low, dark voice that grates down my spine. I swallow hard and take a slow, tentative step away.

"I saved your life," I clamor nervously.

"Why?" he demands angrily. I blink, confused that he would be so angry to be alive. Well, undead alive, I guess.

"Because you saved mine."

His frown deepens, crinkling his forehead, his gaze momentarily off. But when they refocus on me, his eyes turn black with fury. I swallow hard and take several steps away, fear pounding against my ears. Not like his sickly eyes, but certainly like he's going to kill me.

Wait a minute. I know why he's angry. He's recently Animated, confused, and possibly scared. Although that last part is a more far-fetched possibility.

Sympathetically, I explain, "Sometimes, returning as a Risen suppresses the final memories of life that—"

"My memories aren't suppressed," he sneers, and I nod rapidly.

"Okay, okay. Then you understand why I'd want to save your life when you saved me from the Gargoyles." Even though I'm the Mistress, I don't understand why I'm as confused as he is. If his memories aren't suppressed, then why is he so mad?

14

Kilian stares at me with cold incredulity and snarls; his lips curled, baring his fangs. My body trembles, then jumps away when he spats a word in a language I've never heard but recognize. It's Esperanto, the ancient Vampire language that connects all Vampires to one another. Well, that's according to the theories of Bram Stoker's unpublished letters. A part of me, that part of my brain that thinks like a linguist, catalogs the information for later research.

"You humans are so *stupid*!"

He bellows, snapping me back into a more dangerous present. I flinch but am silently grateful he called me human. Though my gifts categorize me as a Supernatural, I know about them, but I've never had any experiences with Supernaturals. My gratitude is extremely short-lived when Kilian leans closer, his fangs dripping with paralyzing venom.

"I wasn't saving your life!" he yells in disgust. "I was sent to eliminate the Necromancer Suriya Rovana. The Gargoyles were probably sent to stop me!"

My body goes cold in shock, my breath caught between a gasp and a scream. Eliminate me?

"But why?"

"You wouldn't understand," Kilian grumbles with disgust, then mutters the foreign word, which doesn't require me to be a scholar linguist to interpret that it's most likely a curse.

"Tell me, anyway," I order, and he scowls, the silent version of a snarl. The strong angles on his face I'd appreciated earlier while he was unconscious take on a horrific countenance that doesn't make him look any less sexy, just more dangerous.

"No!" he growls.

Taken aback by his refusal, I quickly analyze Nana's lessons about Risen being incapable of disobeying the power of Necromancer masters. Yet, Kilian just disobeyed his Mistress's order. Could Nana have been wrong?

My mind whirls in rapid succession, assessing possible reasons he refused my order, categorizing the possibilities that supernatural Risen might be able to resist control because they're not as susceptible as humans. Maybe Vampire Risen are capable of such strong will because they themselves have the power to mesmerize and, perhaps, their brains have built-in barriers that…

"Where are we?" Kilian interrupts with a startling bark, taking in my small, bare apartment with his judgmental eyes the color of silver again. I frown at his rudeness. My apartment may be small and shabby but clean and orderly. Before I get all snippy with him, awareness of the purpose of his question slams into me, jumpstarting the thumping in my heart. The question wasn't one of arrogance but of placement.

I take a slow, steadying breath and answer, "My apartment?" I cringe that the response sounds like a question, and his frown darkens with suspicion, his steely eyes fixed on mine.

"How did we get here?"

I take another step away because I can't tell him the truth. He can't know I Blinked us back, especially if he was sent to kill me for being an Animator. He'll let others know I'm a Blinker, too, and then they'll kill me even if he no longer can.

Aislynn!

She'll save me! Vampires hate cats, the guardians of the Netherworld, and all that ancient history! I can make my escape by grabbing her as she claws Kilian's face off and Blink us both to the car.

I whistle lightly through trembling lips, and Aislynn jumps from the windowsill, sauntering toward me in her slow I'm-only-coming-because-I-choose-to motion, and I want to scream for her to hurry up. I can order it as her Mistress, but I've never done that to her. It just feels wrong since she's been with me since birth.

I hold Kilian's glare as Aislynn approaches, waiting for him to screech or hiss, or at least jump away. But I grunt my frustration when all she does is brush past my leg toward Kilian and wrap her black tail around his ankle, purring loudly.

Kilian breaks eye contact to glance at the treacherous cat. He instantly looks as confused as I am that she isn't ripping his face off and stares at her for long seconds before he squats to pet her.

She purrs even louder, and I want to kick both out of my apartment with a kick in each ass!

Aislynn lifts her head to his palm and licks it. Kilian inhales sharply in surprise and rubs his fingers over her head, gently tugging at her ears, which she loves because she purrs even louder! I never knew she loved it, but the Vampire seems to have her pegged even though Vampires are supposed to be deathly afraid of cats.

17

Kilian's memories flash in my mind as he realizes he hasn't touched a cat in over four-hundred-years. A memory of a similar cat floats to mind, but Kilian is younger, a frail boy with dark hair that contrasts sharply with pale skin, sallow gray eyes, and thin limbs. His emotions churn with longing as he fondly pets Aislinn, who resembles the one he had as a child.

"Salem." That's the cat's name, and I smile.

But my smile dies when Kilian turns his gold haze and asks harshly, "What did you say?" I stare because I didn't realize I'd spoken the cat's name out loud. Of course, how would I know that unless I can read his mind, which I can't!

I exhale dramatically, quickly grab Aislynn from beneath his legs, and say, "Look. I could've left while your body caught up with your brain's electrical pulses, but I stayed to give you the code."

He frowns, and I continue before he loses his patience or I lose my courage.

"First, you cannot physically hurt me, no matter how much you try. Your intent to do it when you awoke ended at my first command. Second, you obey every one of my directives, whether you agree with them or not. You don't have to worry about that because I'm not sticking around to force too much on you. And third, your life ends when mine does. I shared a part of my essence with you. If my essence expires, it expires within you as well."

Actually, I'm not sure if that's entirely true since an essence is essentially one's soul, and Vampires don't have souls. He doesn't have to know I'm just speculating, though. Kilian does look baffled, and I almost feel sorry for him.

Almost. I'm not stupid enough to think he deserves my compassion and pity. Instead of consoling him, I end with a flair of my hand in the air and, "I have to go now. Farewell, Kilian Willingham. May I never see you in the afterlife."

Chapter 3: Crowded (Suri)

I close my eyes and Blink out of the apartment and into the backseat of my car. But, dammit, I hadn't considered the unnatural speed of Vampires, one in particular who grabbed my bicep when I'd teleported.

Aislynn yowls, and I squeal when Kilian's body slams into mine, and the driver's seat flattens against the car's wheel. He lifts me to a sitting position and straddles my hips in one quick move, his chest pressed on mine. In any other circumstance, I would've been ecstatic that a hot guy was groping me in the back of my Audi.

This is *not* that circumstance!

Kilian robs me of breath, and his hands are wrapped around my wrists so tightly I whimper. His eyes are black orbs of anger so palpable that he physically emits heat. Then he does something so unexpected—as if this entire night isn't enough! I'm frozen in place, staring and trembling. His eyes are no longer the black eyes of a hungry Vampire or the sickly ones I'd seen earlier. His eyes are so humanly filled with emotion that it catches me off guard, and I swallow hard because I don't know what that means.

"How do you know my name?" he asks quietly, completely contradicting the heat coming off him like the fires of the netherworld.

How do I answer him, though? I've just revealed my second gift by assuming I'd just Blink in front of him, and he'd spend the next day — or lifetime — searching for me. By then, I would've been long gone and a distant memory.

Instead, he knows I'm an Animator and a Blinker. If I tell him I also have the gift of Psychometry, there's nowhere in the world I could hide without a supernatural Court of any race searching for me. Kilian may not be able to kill me, but he can sell me out to the highest bidder!

Kilian loosens his hold on my wrist and slightly lifts his weight, giving me more room to breathe, but doesn't release me.

"No one alive knows that name," he continues, his eyes narrow slits of suspicion. "And only one undead who knows it."

His Sire.

My heart hammers when he leans his head toward me, staring at the apex between neck and shoulder blade, then lifts black orbs filled with hunger. He closes his eyes and growls low, a dangerous animal that's finally caught its prey.

"Yet, somehow, *you* know it," he continues, each word slower than the one before it. My body trembles beneath him, which I'm sure he can feel, and he leans closer, his lips too close to my neck.

He can't drain you, I remind myself as calmly as possible. *He can't harm you.* But my heart isn't exactly listening to my comforting words.

I shiver when his breath fans the soft skin and marvel that his breath smells like nothing. I bet mine smells like I haven't brushed it in over twenty-four hours, which is a winning possibility.

I whimper when he drags the tips of his fangs down my neck, and I repeat my mantra.

He can't drain you.

He can't harm you.

He can't drain you.

He can't harm you.

His intimidation, though, feels scarier than what he *can* do.

Kilian breathes in deeply and growls, "I'm starving!"

His voice resonates in the small car, and a tear slips from my eye. He leans his teeth into my neck but stops just as the tip of his fangs touch my skin. I close my eyes, trembling like a leaf in a Louisiana storm, repeating my mantra in my head, praying Nana wasn't wrong about this rule like the one about instant obedience.

Kilian's body shakes, too. Not with fear, but with need.

"So why can't I feed from you?" he bellows, pulling more tears from my eyes as his frustration echoes in the cabin. Two nearby car alarms blare around us. I close my eyes from this nightmarish scene because, I swear, I might pee myself if he doesn't get off me. At least, my command to never drink my blood is stronger than Kilian's innate nature.

"Leave me and feed elsewhere, preferably far away from here," I stutter in fright, hoping that it comes off more as a Mistress's command to her Risen than the wishful thinking of a scared-as-hell woman.

Kilian drops his forehead on my shoulder and breathes heavily, occasionally snarling, his body trembling like mine. Though his heart doesn't beat, his breathing mimics my thundering heart. I don't even know how he's holding himself off me so easily because I'm wider than he is, and we're both awkwardly squeezed in my tiny car.

"I'm starving," he whispers, and I'd almost pity him if he wasn't so close to my jugular. "I *need* to feed after an injury, or I'll go into a starvation frenzy, and it'll be *your* fault." He growls the last part, and my pity fizzles and dies in his accusation. I don't understand why he won't just obey my command!

"You won't let me feed from you, and I can't let you go."

"Why not?" I ask urgently because that's *exactly* what I want him to do, and he's not obeying! He's silent for seconds, his loud, heavy breathing echoing in the small vehicle. Despite the near-death circumstances, my mind teases me about how *awesome* it would be to have a sexy man breathing heavily only inches away from my neck would be if he weren't a starved Vampire struggling with obedience issues.

"Because I've never missed a kill," he clips between clenched fangs. He pulls his head away, his eyes red with carmine darkness, the beast that's way too close to the surface. "I may not be able to feed from you, but I'm not releasing you either."

Kilian shocks me into a scream when he bites down on my shoulder, his fangs ripping through fabric and muscle.

"You can't do that!" I scream in terror, my voice cracking as tears pour out of my eyes as if they were holy water that could banish him. "I ordered it! I ordered it!"

Kilian's fangs immediately pull out, staining my tank-top in the dark red of my blood. I inhale sharply when his tongue licks the blood from my shoulder. His loud, hoarse groan gives voice to my tears, but he continues licking instead of sucking, until the pain is gone and the only sound between us is our breathing. He's healed the wound with his saliva, but he's marked me as well.

Kilian's angry, black eyes meet mine and he says, "Now you cannot hide from me. I've tasted your blood and let you live." I stare at his slightly blurred face between the tears and swallow hard, trying to wrack my brain for information to clarify whether the exchange of blood and saliva is part of the process of Turning, but my studies are more focused on Necromancy, Teleportation, and Psychometry. Not necessarily Vampirism.

Kilian must see the confusion on my face because he smiles coldly. Vicious. Cruel.

"You must be the dumbest Necromancer in the world," he accuses with acerbic mockery, and my cheeks inadvertently flush, like he's slapped me because I don't necessarily disagree. When a Vampire tastes a person's blood, even if it's not for feeding, the blood links the Vampire to the person, thus being able to track the person wherever she goes. I should've ordered him not to *bite* me instead of not *feed* from me.

24

"Your blood will lead me to you so long as it still pumps," he confirms. "And my Vampire nature will seek it until it consumes it."

I stare wide-eyed because he's the one who doesn't know what he just did, but I do! Not only is his Vampire blood-bound to me, but he would also be bound anyway as my Risen. I'm not sure what that kind of double whammy will look like, but I'll never be able to shake off this damned Vampire Risen!

Kilian doesn't give me enough time to turn my own bitterness against him because he leans his face into mine, his eyes taking on a steely look; the gunmetal shine of a madman rather than just a Vampire, as if Vampire isn't enough! I can't turn away because there isn't enough room to move my head. I hold my breath when his face suddenly softens, and I see Kilian, the man, for the first time. He's more beautiful than just sexy, with sharp features on a lean face, a fine nose that inhales me slowly, and lush lips stained with my blood.

When my eyes stop ogling his beauty, my eyes meet his, the silver somehow glowing in the shadowed car, like they're smiling at me even though his lips aren't.

I smile back stupidly.

"Sleep, Suriya," Kilian whispers, his voice smooth and satiny, like my gloves. "When you wake, you'll have much answering to do."

I frown. Sleep? I don't want to sleep. I want to stare into Kilian's eyes and watch them glow in the dark, mercury in moonlight. He says something else, and I blink slowly, trying to capture the words, but they're butterflies around my head, sounds and colors I can't catch.

When his cold hand grazes my cheek, fear crashes into me, breaking the spell. His eyes are cold steel again. I try to thrash against him when the beautiful face turns into an ugly scowl. He orders me to sleep with so much force the world narrows to a single point: his eyes blazing like mercury on fire, before everything turns blurry, then black.

Chapter 4: The Risen (Kilian)

Rage and fury war with indignation and the kind of frustration that blisters the gums around my fangs. But the truth of my own failure makes me see red.

Literally.

Emotions, often so well-hidden no one can gauge them, literally drive me back to the estate in the Necromancer's miniature Audi. The small, compact car adds to my anger, forcing me to push the seat back as far as it goes without killing the portly Necromancer. Still, I can barely fold my long legs to drive properly, and discarding belongings from the backseat so that she'd fit doesn't make the ride any more bearable.

Her cat, the one that looks exactly like Salem, sits on my lap for the entire ride, purring loudly and rubbing against my hand like I'm not a starving, raving mad Vampire who might eat it as an appetizer.

Not that I eat animals.

My stomach cramps so tightly from lack of blood that my head pounds along with the rhythm of *her* heart, *her* blood, *her* bloody essence, which is probably the only reason I'm following the human part of me that isn't predatory enough to hunt for food out in the open.

Because *she's* here!

When I finally arrive at the estate, I can barely think about anything but feeding, except sneaking the stupid Necromancer in my bedchamber through the window so no one sees my failure to kill her. I dump her on the king-size bed and stalk out of my room, slamming the door, knowing she won't wake from the mesmer until I wake her, and then I go on the prowl for housepets.

I growl when, instead of finding a pet along the dark hallway decorated in floor-to-ceiling burgundy drapes, Tyran finds me.

"You don't look so well," he comments with blithe disregard to my obvious state of starvation, and I ram my shoulder into his.

"Find me a suitable housepet," I demand, but he quickly blocks my path, his eyes taking in the gravity of my request.

"You look starved, Kilian," he observes cautiously, and his sudden concern annoys the hell out of me. I'd rather he be the annoyingly cheerful nuisance he can be than the worried big brother he actually is. "Your eyes are starving red."

I glare at him because that's exactly what I am right now!

"What happened?"

I snarl with the aggression of a frustrated and ravenous Vampire, not wanting to admit my failure, my unexpected death, and my unwanted resurrection. The response startles Tyran, his bright blue eyes glowing with shock. I curse in Esperanto and growl as I pass Tyran.

"Just find me a pet!"

"From the looks of it, you'll kill the pet," Tyran points out accurately. I'm so hungry I won't be able to stop the feeding frenzy that'll take over. "I'll get you three, but I'm coming with you."

"I can feed myself!"

"I know you can," he says calmly. "But you'll kill all three if unsupervised." My fangs burn against my gums, so I nod just to get fed. If I kill another housepet, Court Celosia will cancel my contract and banish me!

I lead Tyran to the mansion's right wing, where the housepets are housed. He keeps pace, but he's known me long enough to keep his mouth shut and his queries to himself. When we reach the wing, and I push the doors wide open, Tyran rushes ahead and knocks on the third door to the left. Celyn's door. My preferred housepet.

Tyran peers into her room and speaks in hushed tones as I approach like a predator ready to pounce. The door swings wider, and Celyn stands at the door, completely naked, her breasts bouncing with each beat of her anxious heart.

I don't bother facing Tyran when I order, "Find me two more." I hold Celyn's frightened brown eyes to mine for only short seconds before I rush her, grab her by the waist, pull her flush against my chest, and sink my fangs into her neck with a bite. I'm too hungry to deliver the toxins that'll give her pleasure.

Instead, she screams, which she's never done before. Warm blood gushes into my mouth and down my constricted throat. I groan at the taste, the smell, the very texture begging me for more as I suck deeper. Celyn inhales sharply, her blood pumping into major organs and cells, rehydrating them.

I lift my head and snarl. The pain from the swelling organs and cells crashes into my other bodily systems. We're both breathing heavily, Celyn holding back her whimpers because she's an experienced housepet, and me breathing in her fear, reawakening the beast within me.

I sink my fangs back into her neck, and she screams again, then whimpers a plea I can't hear past the gushing of her blood in my mouth, more precious than her pathetic begging. When her head flops to one side, Tyran grabs the back of my neck and forcefully yanks me off Celyn. I hiss aggressively at his intrusion as the pet's body thumps to the ground.

I grab the housepet Tyran replaces for Celyn and drop my head to her neck, my fangs unceremoniously latching onto her jugular. The housepet screams and thrashes, spurring the predator in me even more as I suck in her blood, roughly tilting her head for easier access. This pet's salty tears mingle with the coppery taste of blood. I lift my fangs with a feral growl of pleasure.

Tyran takes that moment of brief unlatching to yank me away before the pet dies. Snarling with each breath and swaying from the fading of adrenaline and blood-frenzy, Tyran passes me another pet. This one is younger, thinner, with frightened mud-brown eyes and a small mouth that trembles. She glances from me to the other, more experienced and unconscious housepets and sobs with unpatterned wails.

Disgusted, I push her away while Tyran licks the other pet's wound before she bleeds out. He's most likely done the same for

Celyn, which pleases me because her body is as pleasing as her blood.

But not as sweet as the Necromancer's.

I don't care enough about the housepets like Tyran does. Celyn serves me and it would be a disadvantage for her to die while I feed. But caring about her life is like a farmer naming his cows, knowing they'll be led to the slaughter someday.

Not that Court Celosia would willingly allow the slaughter of its housepets. While it happens every so often with over-eager fledglings and starved Ancients during Waking, the Vampire Court Council frowns upon hurting volunteer housepets who feed Vampires, especially since the Supernatural Courts Council, or SupaCourt, has forbidden the hunting of humans to minimize exposure. As a Vampire Huntsman, I hunt whatever I want, including targets.

Targets like Necromancers.

With a disgusted grunt, I lurk away and head back to the residential wing, back to my bedchamber where I can face my Necromancer problem, fully fed.

"Hunter!" Tyran calls after me, and I exhale heavily because I know he'll ask questions and want details, and I'll have to give it to him because he'll keep asking them until I want to drain *his* blood dry!

Tyran may be older than me by over two-thousand years, but he's no longer ruthless. We used to be Huntsmen together as part of the Black Hearts Unit before we were disbanded when hunting became forbidden. Tyran chose to spend the rest of his days

31

protecting the Vampire community from human detection and possible annihilation in hopes of joining the SupaCourt someday. He's definitely much better at dealing with politics and people, both natural and supernatural, than I am.

I'm a trained killer of humans *and* Supernaturals, Necromancers being my specialty. I'm *not* a social Vampire. No one in Court Celosia approaches me unless they absolutely must, and even then, it's through Tyran, who's more sociable than I am. The only time Jocasta, the head Court Councilman, spoke to me was to assign the hunt of Suriya Rovana.

The one who escaped with *my* life!

I growl just as Tyran catches up to me, his eyes so full of questions that his mouth can barely keep shut. But we won't speak until we reach my bedchamber. We've learned from working in other courts that no one is to be trusted in any court, Vampire or otherwise, since we don't really belong to any.

I'm a hired assassin who stays in any given Court only long enough to find and eliminate Necromancers, and Tyran is my handler. Since he's the only one I trust, he often accompanies me for the purpose of networking with the Vampire Courts Council and councilmen of other races. We only speak freely in our chambers after we've swept the rooms for listening devices, then added scramblers so no one can listen in on our conversations, not even Supernaturals.

"Your chin is dripping blood all over the expensive, though ghastly, carpeting," Tyran comments with a blithe smirk. "Just a little speck, right there." He points to the right side of my mouth and chuckles. His humor is forced, though only I would notice. He's putting on a show for the multiple cameras that line the hallway. I ignore him with a scowl, playing my part in our macabre performance for the curious and cunning, Vampire qualities of envy and wariness.

When we enter the opulent bedchamber and close the ears and eyes of the unwelcomed eavesdroppers, Tyran drops the act and questions seriously, "What happened? Was it the mission?"

I turn to him in exasperation and point in the direction of the bed. He follows my finger, then his eyes widen. He glances back at me, increased concern and shock in his sea-green eyes, and back at the Necromancer, who hasn't woken.

"Is she human?" I nod, and he frowns.

"But… I can't smell her."

"Precisely the reason Jocasta sent *me* to complete the mission and not Tanith, who'd already failed them twice. The Necromancer was very hard to track because she doesn't smell human."

"Necromancers smell like dry, compact earth, but she doesn't smell like anything," Tyran adds with confusion but also intrigue. "She just smells like… *you*."

"Of course she does," I say with irritation. "She's in my chamber." He turns his baffled expression to me and presses.

"But there's no human scent *beneath* yours. How is that even possible?" I turn away, wiping blood from my chin with the sleeve of a black button-down shirt. I can't answer his question because I don't really know why she doesn't smell human.

"If this is the Necromancer," Tyran asserts with a tilt of his head and narrowing of his eyes, "then that means you failed your mission?"

"And died failing at it," I reveal dryly. His eyes grow wide again, and he turns to the unconscious Necromancer, then back at me, and curses in English.

He no longer speaks Esperanto, even though he's much older than me. He'd rather speak English, even though it's a bastard descendant of the Germanic language.

"She's your Mistress then," he concludes quietly, turning back to the chamber door as if someone might still be able to hear us. Our hearing is acute enough to know there isn't anyone out there.

Yet.

"Do you know the Risen Code?" he asks, adding to the grave solemnity of my situation, a death knell. I turn to the Necromancer, small but plump, like a ripe grape just waiting to be sucked dry. I shake my head in response to Tyran's question.

"She mentioned something about not being able to hurt her, which is why I didn't drain *her* blood like I wanted to do. But I was too angry, and even hungrier, to focus on the rest of the rules."

"Kilian," Tyran says in a sigh, pushing his blonde hair away from his face with his fingers; a messy look Kali seems to like.

"Did she command you to not drink her blood?" I nod, then shake my head.

"Not exactly in those words," I clarify. "She said I can't feed from her without her permission." Tyran nods pensively.

"The first rule is that you cannot hurt her after giving her first command, which she did. The second one is that you must obey everything she orders you to do."

"I disobeyed her when she ordered me to leave."

"Why did she order you to leave?" I glance at him and shrug. Tyran looks stumped. "What Necromancer dismisses her own Risen?" I shrug, unbuttoning the soiled black shirt. "How is it that she ended up unconscious on your bed?"

"Mesmered," I reveal, which deepens his confusion.

"I didn't think that would be possible if she's your Mistress." I flinch.

"Have you heard of any other Vampires becoming Risen?" I ask, almost eagerly because, if there are records of Vampires who've been animated, then I won't be the first careless Vampire who managed to document the experience.

"Not in any of the annals," Tyran says, deflating my hope. I pause, real concern tasting acrid in my mouth, then inhale deeply and reveal my concern.

"She knew my name," I said quietly, her knowledge of it causing deeper concern.

"Hunter?" I shake my head.

"I purposely named myself something else to conceal my human identity," I remind him, since it had been his original idea. "But she called me Kilian Willingham."

He frowns deeply and steps away to pace and think. Tyran is a thinker whereas I'm a doer. While I'm not impulsive, I'd rather act than think about it. I leave those details to Tyran.

"How would she know your given name, the one given to you by your parents? The one no one knows, except for me." I don't reply because I don't know.

Tyran paces slowly, trying to make sense of this intriguing mystery while I remain plagued by having failed, died, and become a Risen to a Necromancer who already knows too much about me.

Tyran stops, looks at the Necromancer with furrowed brow, and slowly ambles to the bed. Instantly, my chest tightens with apprehension. The reaction is unfamiliar and unwelcome because Tyran is the only person I trust with my life. I scowl when he deeply inhales her scent and shakes his head in confusion.

"I need a shower," I mutter awkwardly, removing my clothing while I enter the spacious bathroom adjacent to the chamber and turn on the shower. As I step into the cold water, I run my hand through my dark hair, the water instantly curling it. I wipe my face, blood staining the clear water as it cascades down my body to my feet and disappears into the drain in morbid swirls of pink.

I curse quietly, an ancient Esperanto word that's older, less vulgar, but more finite. Not only does it insult the problem, but it also eliminates any possibility of a solution.

How did I get myself into this mess? I'd smelled the Gargoyles on my back but needed to keep my eyes on the Necromancer or I'd lose her again. It had already taken me weeks to track her to the private university and, without a scent, I had to rely on my other senses. My focus hadn't been on why she had no smell. That's more Tyran's area of expertise.

My focus was on hunting her, regardless of the details. But the Gargoyles had caught up, their stone-and-mortar distorting, assaulting my senses. Then they shot four consecutive wooden stakes, the kind that burned like hell and left a hole the size of an American dime. There must have been four Gargoyles, each shooting a stake because one penetrated my heart just as the Necromancer turned to face me.

While I may tell Tyran that something had changed in me the moment I awoke as a Risen, it had been the moment something changed in the depths of the wide brown eyes. As my back burned into the ashes of my existence, her eyes brightened to amber, as if a light had been lit behind her eyeballs. Then she placed her hand on mine, and I died.

Well, more appropriately, I lost consciousness.

The death of a Vampire lasts no more than five seconds, closer to three. It's almost instantaneous. But the way the Necromancer had held my gaze, captured it, not with expected horror or fear, but with surprise and redemption, hope and a gift. Her eyes had derailed me from finishing her off with me. I should've ripped her throat open within those three seconds, and I would've succeeded at my mission.

But her eyes had ambushed me, and I failed to finish her off and ended up turning into a Risen for the wrong reason!

I turn the shower off and lean my forehead against the slick wall with eyes closed, water dripping from my hair and down my body. I wipe a hand over my damp face despondently. I've never failed a mission. Not since Father died. Never as a Vampire! I pushed my training as far as I could for the sole purpose of never failing. And now, I've become a servant to the very people I trained to assassinate.

A jolt of panic hits my chest so drastically I place my hand over it, my heart pounding underneath. Something hot burns in my bones, as if a match had been lit in the marrow, setting it on fire. The Necromancer's frightened face flashes in my eyes, her fear becoming mine. I jump out of the shower, nearly slip on the bathroom tiles when an uncomfortable and foreign shiver of fear titters along my skin.

When I scent it in the air, I slam open the bathroom door, and rush to the bedchamber where the Necromancer stares at Tyran wide-eyed and pale, her fear tapping a rhythm against my chest. I scowl at Tyran even though he's just sitting at the edge of the bed furthest from her, watching her, deep in thought.

The Necromancer turns her brown eyes to me; the brightness returning so that the brown is more burnt honey, glistening. I hold her gaze, or perhaps more accurately, she holds mine. I can't look away, drawn by its pull, and it feels like I'm mesmerized by her. The bedchamber, the bed, and even Tyran fade into the background. My mind solely focused on her. She's as captivated as I am, except that she's the one holding the control I can't reject. I'm so used to being the one in control—mind and body—that I'm surprised I'm so drawn to her.

When she breaks eye contact, I release a breath, blinking the unease. Her eyes, brown and soft again, move from my face, down my body, and back up, her cheeks flushing pink, then red.

In a flurry of shock and embarrassment, she covers her face with her hands and shrieks, "Why are you naked?"

I glance at Tyran, ready to confront his amusement, but he's staring at me with the serious coldness that makes him an Ancient Vampire. He may seem carefree and lighthearted, but he's no less dangerous and cunning than any other Vampire. More so. Just like no one else knows my given name, no one knows his real age but me.

Even so, I scowl, daring him to make a move that'll prove I'm more a Black Heart than he is, despite his age. He may be faster and stronger than me, but he's gone soft, which is his choice, and I've only gotten harder, darker, which is mine.

He must interpret my scowl correctly because Tyran shrugs and tells me lightly, "Well, go put some clothes on." I snarl, and the tightness in my chest increases. I whip my angry gaze to the Necromancer, who's visibly trembling.

"Are you afraid of me, Necromancer?" I ask gravely. I want her to know that I would kill her if I weren't Risen-bound to her! She raises her amber eyes to mine; the honey turning brown again. She frowns and drops her head back into her hands.

"No, Risen," she muffles behind her fingers. "I'm not afraid of you."

"Don't call me that!" I demand angrily, approaching her dangerously.

39

"Then don't call me Necromancer," she argues. "We're called Animators, and I also have a name, Kilian."

"Don't call me that either!" I bellow, and Tyran quickly interjects brightly, "Hi, Ms. Animator. My name is Tyran Kane. I'm Hunter's best friend." I grunt, not because he's not my closest friend, but because that's more information than she deserves. I head to the armoire to find clothes while Tyran waits for her name.

She doesn't bother looking up when she says, "Suri."

"Suriya," I retort. Trying to find a Suri *Rovan* had been impossible until my search turned up Rovana, then Suriya.

She lifts her head to shoot me an indignant look and warns, "You don't get to call me that if I don't get to call you Kilian."

"Is that an order?" I ground out between clenched teeth, anger simmering close to my skin. "Or a request?"

"Neither! It's a clarification." Tyran snickers, and I glare at him, but he addresses the Necromancer.

"You see, Suri, I am the only person who knows his given name, and Hunter, as he is known, would prefer it that way." I return to the bathroom and pull a towel from the rack, drying the water droplets still clinging to my skin. I'm pulled back into the room, uncomfortable leaving the Necromancer with Tyran, even though there's no reason for my paranoia.

"Fine," she mumbles. "Is he dressed?" I frown and grab a black fitted T-shirt and black slacks as Tyran smiles with amusement. Sometimes he's the most frustrating Vampire in existence. And sometimes, he's exactly what I need to stave the deep darkness away.

"Why do his eyes change so often?" she asks curiously. Her curiosity annoys me.

"Because our eyes reflect our feeding needs," Tyran explains, and the Necromancer adds, "And emotions." I frown and put the clothes on, cross my arms, and glare at her.

"Okay, he's dressed," Tyran says amiably, and she pulls her hands away, immediately finding my eyes. Tyran and I smell fear on her even though her expression is almost neutral, except for the uncanny brightness of her eyes, shining with authority and allure.

I hate them!

"So," Tyran begins, moving around the bed closer to her. She follows his movements, pulls the edge of her bottom lip into her mouth, then looks at me. Strangely, I'm transfixed by the soft intake of her breath, the slight scratching of her teeth on her lip, the way she softly sucks on it. Our eyes meet for a split second before Tyran continues talking.

It only takes that split moment to know that, though her expression is blank, she's just pretending to not be afraid. Her fear is an ugly snake slithering just under my skin where no one can see it. I absently scratch my forearm, barely able to hide my discomfort and unease. Not of her. But, more worrisome, of Tyran.

Chapter 5: The Ternion (Kilian)

"Do your hands have some kind of skin disease?" The Necromancer and I both look at Tyran in equal confusion.

"No," she replies slowly.

"Interesting," he comments with small, pensive nods. He doesn't explain the reason for his odd question, and I wonder what he's getting at.

"What's interesting?" the Necromancer asks, falling for Tyran's bait. She's either really dumb or incredibly innocent, unaware of the supernatural world even though she's somewhat of a supernatural herself.

"That your hand isn't deformed, and yet you wear satin gloves as if you were a museum conservator." I turn to her and notice the satin gloves even though she's wearing a pair of gray sweatpants, tight around her large thighs, a loose sweater torn at the shoulder where I bit her, and fuzzy socks.

"So what?" she says defensively, crossing her arms over her girth.

Interesting.

"Well," Tyran continues coolly, slowly edging closer. Her fear jacks up, and the allusive snake raises its sharp scales under my skin. I ignore it with a hard swallow and a clenching of my jaw. "If you don't have a skin condition on your hands and Vampires don't have viruses, I can't help but wonder why you're wearing gloves."

"Maybe my hands are cold," she retorts irately, anxiety now joining her fear; a slightly different kind of scent radiates from someone with secrets and lies. "Vampires generate their own heat, so they don't need it like we do."

"Your hands are cold." Tyran grins with cunning, which only unnerves her more. She's just revealed that she knows enough about us not to be fooled. So why hide her fear when we can scent it? Maybe it's a natural human reaction in the face of supernatural danger.

"Why do you care about my hands?" she adds testily. Tyran's grin widens, and it looks more predatory than friendly.

"What are you hiding?" I snap impatiently, not as adept at playing with the mouse as Tyran is. "You're already a Necromancer and a Blinker."

"Animator!" she snaps back at the same time Tyran blurts, "A Blinker?"

Tyran's eyes bore into me, but I keep my eyes on the Necromancer as she frowns. A thought forms in my head, one that is more dangerous than just having failed at killing her, one Tyran assuredly picks up on as well because he's more devious than I am and has more to gain than I do.

I smile darkly, startling her as she moves away from where Tyran and I are standing, biting her lip again. I stare at the glimpse of her pink tongue before it disappears. I wish she'd stop distracting me with the habit!

"I know how you know my name," I tell her. "And I know why you don't smell human."

"You will reveal it to no one," she quickly orders, and I growl as the word of what she is sticks to the roof of my mouth but doesn't leave its place there. I hiss at her and angrily crawl on the bed, reaching for her neck. I can't hurt her, but I sure as hell can scare her!

She scurries away with a shriek and falls off the bed with a loud thump. Even so, she jumps back up despite her clumsy size, slamming her back against the chamber door.

She turns to open it, but Tyran calmly advises, "You're in the Celosia Vampire Court, Suri. This bedchamber is the only safe place in the entire mansion for you. I don't recommend opening that door."

The Necromancer turns to face us again when Tyran suggests, "Why don't you tell us how you know Hunter's given name and why you don't have a natural scent." She stares at Tyran, then turns her attention to me, holding my eyes with so much intensity I'm lost in them again. They're captivating, bright and beautiful, like the orange hues of a sunrise I barely tolerate. While I know what she's doing, I can't tear my eyes away from hers, mesmerized by their beauty, their softness, the allure that draws me to her.

Tyran calls my name, but it's distant, muffled by my inability to tear my eyes from the Necromancer's. When he calls me by my given name, I slowly turn to him, as if time has slowed to a crawl and the only one that matters within its grasp is the Necromancer.

Tyran snaps his fingers, and I blink away the Necromancer's mesmer. I growl and turn angry red eyes in her direction. My fangs dropping from the anger of her control. She startles, and her fear hits me so hard it takes my breath away. I despise her more because I can't move from where I stand. My body stiffens, frozen in place, and I snarl with immobile rage. She stares with untethered fear, the stink only driving me to fury.

Tyran drops his calm, friendly demeanor and shows the Necromancer the Vampire he really is. "He may not be able to kill you, but I'm fast enough to do it myself without his being able to stop me."

"You'll kill him, too, if you do," she remarks quickly, her voice shaky but determined even though her amber eyes haven't released mine. "If my life ends, so does his when my essence fades inside him. We're literally ashes to ashes." She turns her attention to Tyran, and I nearly collapse at the break in eye contact. I glare at her from hooded, narrowed eyes.

"I'm not afraid of either of you. I know you're his good friend, possibly his only friend, because he really isn't a nice guy, whereas you at least try to be. So you won't kill me because you won't kill him." Tyran smiles, but it's cold and dangerous.

"I can hurt you, though," he continues coolly. "I can hurt you until you wish for death, and it will not be given for the very reason you just shared."

His words startle me, not because he isn't capable of doing exactly what he says, but because the threat hits me with a wall of protective violence.

The Necromancer lifts her head confidently and replies, "He won't let you."

Tyran turns to me, his expression darkening, his features harsh and ancient. I don't know what he sees, but I can't stop my reaction just as much as I can't move from where the Necromancer has me rooted. When Tyran's eyes turn completely black, flecks of fire red revealing his true form, closer to the surface than I've seen in a long time, I drop my gaze. Not in fear, but in respect.

Tyran turns black eyes to the Necromancer and admits in a haughty, authoritative voice, "We're at an impasse." I raise my eyes in surprise. I've never heard Tyran speak this way and watch as he stares the Necromancer down with a cold, calculating glare.

"His Sire versus his Mistress," she whispers, to Tyran's surprise.

I expel the heavy breath I'd been holding for centuries between clenched teeth. Tyran has never mentioned his Sireship, and I've never brought it up. We've always just been friends.

Until now.

"I know who you are," she reveals in a tremulous voice, her arms wrapped around her girth, recognizing Tyran for the Vampire Ancient he is. "I've seen you in his memories." My hunch is correct, and it worries me a lot more than pitting her against Tyran.

"Psychometric Seer," Tyran confirms in slow, pointed syllables. "A soul seer. That's why your hands are covered. Your touch exposes you to past memories, thoughts, and emotions of the person you touch. Their deepest, darkest secrets laid bare to you."

"As if I'd experienced them myself," she whispers, almost sadly, turning her glistening gaze to me, blinking back tears. I'm not sure if the tears are for what she's seen in my past, or for what I've experienced. "Even with soulless creatures."

Tyran turns his dispassionate expression to me and clarifies, "*Your* memories, Kilian. *Your* thoughts and *your* emotions." I scowl.

"Listen," the Necromancer interjects, finding her voice again. "I'm not getting in the middle of your relationship, whatever it is. It's clear Kilian sees you more as a friend than a Sire, and you've treated him as such in his memories. I'll just be on my way, and you can remain friends without my interference. I'm not interested in being his Mistress since that had been my mistake for sorely misjudging his reason for jumping in front of wooden stakes. So, if you'll just lead me out… uh, safely, I'll get out of your court."

Tyran exhales, and I feel his tension and mine release in that one breath. "You're right, Suri. Kilian is more to me than a subordinate youngling. He's like a brother." His words warm me, and I turn away, embarrassed by the sudden emotion stuffed in my throat like cotton balls. It's the first time he's ever spoken of his fondness, though he's cared about me since before the Turning.

"Great," she breathes, the smile in her voice causing me to lift my eyes to hers. They're a caramel brown again, shimmering with relief.

But it's short-lived because Tyran adds, "But I can't let you leave."

"What?" she shrieks. She looks from him to me and back to Tyran in confusion and horror. "Why not?"

"Because there are only three Ternions every three generations, and you are one of them," Tyran explains. "A Ternion hasn't been revealed in three generations. Until now. Until you." The Necromancer is shaking her head, her anxiety peaking so high it's practically choking me. "It also means that there are two more yet to be discovered."

"Please don't do this," she begs quietly.

"Only if you sever your ties to Kilian," Tyran bargains coolly. She blinks rapidly and shakes her head again.

"I-I don't know how to do that. He's…" Her eyes move around the room, another indication that she's hiding something else. Until they meet mine again.

"He's what?" Tyran presses while I force myself not to fall for her mesmer again.

"He's… my only Risen. I've… I've never Risen anyone else." She pauses and her eyes widen, like she just had a frightening thought. As if being held captive in a Vampire court isn't frightening enough. "Where's Aislynn?"

"Who?" I ask gruffly.

"My cat. Where's my cat? Did you leave her in the apartment? No. I had her in my arms when we got in the car." She gasps. "Did you squish her when we were in the car? Oh my God, did you kill her? Because if you didn't, she'll tear the door down searching for me!"

Her comment piques my curiosity and I say, "Why would a cat do that? It's not like she's going to starve after a few hours."

"Cats don't starve," Tyran chimes in. "They hunt."

"You would know," I chide, and Tyran chuckles. He's set his eyes on a jaguar shifter who wants nothing to do with him. She's tried to kill him several times, eager to get him off her back so she can find a compatible mate. They've been at it for a couple of decades now, leading nowhere for either of them.

"This is *not* a laughing matter!" the Necromancer interrupts testily, tugging at the gloves, and I raise an eyebrow at the anger and indignation scenting the room. "My cat! Where is she?"

"You didn't answer why she'd tear through a door to find you," Tyran reminds her. She frowns and looks down at her gloved hands.

"Because she's a Risen," she says quietly, and I can't hold back my surprise, or Tyran his condescending chuckle.

"So, you do have a Risen," Tyran states.

She scowls and says, "A cat is *not* the same as a man."

"A Vampire," I clarify dryly. Tyran steps away and begins slowly from bedside to chamber door and back. I watch with growing discomfort because Tyran only paces when he's thinking about something that has him stumped. But what does a Risen cat have to do with me?

While he thinks, I mock crudely, "As a Ternion, why don't you have a harem of Risen at your beck and call?" Her ruddy face reddens again before it darkens with livid indignation.

"I'm *not* the kind of woman to take advantage of others."

"Is there any other kind of woman?" I taunt, though I'm only baiting her. She doesn't take the bait. "In other words, you don't know how to use your gifts well enough to be *that* kind of woman."

"I do know how to use them, very well," she emphasizes, the authority in her voice biting my words. "I was *raised* not to use them for my own gain, which is why I only have one Risen." She pauses and frowns again. "Well, two, with you."

"A cat and a Vampire," I point out as a laconic insult, unable to hide the indignation from my tone. "Clearly not to your own gain." She drops her gaze to her gloves again, another bad habit. She frowns, obviously regretting having saved me. For some reason, that bothers me more than it should, considering I don't want to be her Vampire Risen!

I almost growl when she sucks the bottom side of her lip and nibbles at it. I turn my attention to Tyran, so I don't have to visualize the taste of them. Tyran stops pacing, leaving me expectant of his next words.

"You've only turned a cat into a Risen. Is the cat attached to you, protective and possessive?"

She nods vigorously and says, "Yes! Very much so! Not only because she's been with me since I was three years old, but because she's my Risen." I'm taken aback by the cat's age, but also by what Tyran is implying.

He turns his keen eyes on me, and I curse.

"I am *not* a cat!"

"You're not human either," he argues coolly, and I flash angry eyes at the only human in the room. I stalk toward her until my legs freeze again, short feet from her trembling form. I hiss, my fangs filling my mouth with venomous anger.

"I will not become attached to you!"

Her eyes brighten to the amber that captivates me, and I instantly look away even when she replies testily, "I don't want you to become attached to me! I want you to abandon me! But *you* made it worse by tasting my blood!" Tyran regards me with disappointment, hitting me like a silver arrow. I turn my angry expression on the Necromancer.

"Doubly bound," Tyran comments. "A Risen bond and a blood bond."

"Look, I don't want this as much as you don't," the Necromancer insists. "Just return Aislynn to me, and we'll disappear so you can live your undead life however way you please."

"It would please me to suck you dry!" I attack.

"Well, you can't, can you?" she scoffs with a lofty tilt of her chin, and I hiss again.

"Enough," Tyran says gently. "Kilian, you cannot kill her and will probably not let anyone else hurt or kill her, whether you like it or not." I scowl at the blunt truth of his words. "And Suri, we are not just letting you go so we could live our undead lives 'however way we please,' as you so eloquently put it."

"Why?" she whines, and I want to snap her neck in disgust. It reminds me of the brown-eyed housepet with the trembling chin and pathetic tears.

Tyran closes the space between them in a flash, and she begs, "Please don't touch me. Please don't. His memories and experiences are awful enough. I don't want yours. You've been alive for too long! You've lived too much!" Her words take me aback, my chest tightening with knowing that my life of violence and blood affects her. Tyran nods and respects her request by crossing his arms behind his back.

"We cannot release you because you're one of three Ternions: an Animator, Blinker, and, most rare, a Seer." When he leans in, his fangs dropping from his gums to make his point clear, my legs finally move, and I reach Tyran's side so quickly I can barely hold back from grabbing the back of his neck.

"Don't touch her," I snarl involuntarily. Tyran senses the tension in my muscles, his eyes turning inky black. Even so, he raises his palms and steps away.

Relief overwhelms me when he says, "Well, Kilian, your behavior proves that you are a cat, after all." He chuckles at my expense, and winks at Suri, who stares in confusion and apprehension. She slips her lip between her teeth, and I frown. But when her eyes land on mine, it's my turn to hold them, lacing my words with the Vampire power ingrained in me.

"If I'm stuck being your Risen, then you're stuck being my Mistress." I lean in close, desperate to smell her human scent, and disappointed that I only smell mine. "I will *never* let you go, Necromancer, even when we're no longer bound, because you're a Ternion and then you'll become *my* housepet."

To my surprise, she leans in closer, gets on her tiptoes so that we're nose-to-nose close, and replies boldly, "I will find a way to get us out of being bound to each other, then I *will* disappear. I will *never* let you keep me; much less be your pet. And do you know why? Because you are not *my* housepet and never will be." She pauses for emphasis, and it works as I lean closer, nearly touching her nose with mine, her breath fanning my lips, tugging tight in my gut, her heart seductively beating in my ears.

"You're my Risen," she emphasizes, and I step away, like she's slapped me, and frown. I glance at Tyran, who's grinning annoyingly, like a Cheshire cat.

"This is going to be the most fun I've had in all my years of existence," he quips.

"All two-thousand-six-hundred-and-forty-two years of them," Suri grumbles, and Tyran's smile dissolves.

"It's possible, then, to unbind me from you?" I intervene before Tyran has time to get angry that she knows one of his most intimate secrets. I'm worried about what else my memories have revealed about him. About me.

She breathes in with uncertainty, tugging at the gloves again, and says honestly, "I don't know, but I know someone who might."

"Interesting," Tyran remarks quickly, but I know it's his way of controlling the situation again. "Another Ternion?"

She glares at him and says, "You're not coming. The only reason I'm taking Kilian is because he's my Risen and we both want to be free of the other. But I don't trust him, and I sure as hell trust you even less. I know you only through his memories, and you're no less violent than he is." She shakes her head, apprehension and anxiety scenting the air along with her fear.

"You're just more charming and friendlier. But you have more to gain than just Kilian's freedom from bondage. You're cunning where he's violent. You have an agenda, whereas his goal is simple: break free from me. He, at least, must follow the Risen Code that protects me."

She looks at me and adds, "But only until the bond is broken." Her meaning is clear: I will not hesitate to kill her once the bond is broken, and she's right. "But I know how to thwart a Vampire." She tilts her chin up, glaring. "And how to kill one."

"I doubt that, Necromancer," I growl as Tyran says dismissively, "Of course you do."

"Don't call me that," she replies. "Suri is my name."

"I'm coming with you, anyway," Tyran tells her, undaunted by her surmise of us.

"No, you're not!"

"That's not a decision for you to make," Tyran replies coolly.

"Yes, it is," she says with conviction, gingerly moves around him despite her weight, and grabs my forearm with her smaller hand. Her touch startles me, the feel so powerful, so controlling, that I snarl.

She faces Tyran again and says, "Tyran Kane, may I never see you again."

A Blink is all it takes for my bedchamber and Tyran to disappear and the mansion garage to come into focus. I stumble away from the Necromancer who's still holding my forearm, and curse.

"Yeah, to whatever you said," she responds testily, stepping away from me, but fear and anxiety stink the air between us. "Where's Aislynn?" She crosses her arms over her large bosom and glares at me. I'm confused, not only because she teleported us without me even realizing it, but because she brought us to the garage where I hid her car behind my black Roma.

"How did you know the cat would be here?"

"Just take me to her," she replies impatiently, nervously glancing around. I do the same and frown but slip around my Roma to reach her car. I'd left the windows slightly ajar so the cat could breathe, not that I should care, but the bloody cat is warm and friendly, and purrs loudly on my lap, and is soft and soothing. The Necromancer smiles and whistles lightly when the cat meows.

"Hey, fat girl," she coos, opening the door and quickly picking up her cat. She gives the cat a big kiss on the nose that the cat doesn't appreciate and hugs her. I stare with disgust. I will never understand cat people, not even Shapeshifters!

The Necromancer groans, "Oh girl. Look what you've done to my stuff." The interior of the car is ripped to shreds, including the ceiling's lining, car seats, and whatever the Necromancer had in her duffel bag. I threw everything else out. The sight is disturbing. If a cat can do that kind of damage to be with its Mistress, I want to be released from the Necromancer before I become as obsessed as her twenty-six-year-old cat.

When the Necromancer looks over her shoulder, I frown and ask, "Why do you keep looking around?"

"Teleporting leaves a trace of…" She pauses, trying to find the right word in her busy mind. I know what she's referring to, though.

A supernatural wave.

The existence of Supernaturals distorts the fabric of physics and biology, giving us the ability to stretch the mortal limits that apply to humans. A supernatural trace is like a gravitational wave across space, time, and human understanding. Even after we've left a place, there are still ripples of the supernatural that can be felt, even by sensitive humans. A sudden cold breeze. An orb in a video. An inexplicable mist. They call it ghosts and apparitions. We know it as a supernatural wave.

"How long does the wave last?" I ask, now looking around as well. If the Blink wave is followed, everyone in the mansion will know she's here, and I'm sure it's not what we want. Tyran probably wouldn't want that either, since he would rather have Suri as a bargaining chip than an asset to share.

"Can we just leave?" she urges.

I cross my arms and ask suspiciously, "Why are you in such a rush?"

She exhales heavily and insists, "Give me my car keys. I'm out."

"Why don't you just Blink us out of here if you're so freaked out?" I argue stubbornly because I want to leave, too, but not at her command.

"Because the Blink can be followed!" she replies impatiently. "It'll lead straight to where we're going."

"The wave lasts that long?" I've never heard of such a far-reaching wave.

"Yes! The power of the trace depends on the number of times the supernatural uses a gift, or gifts, or on the power of the supernatural. The more gifts, the more power. The more power, the longer the wave."

"And you're a Ternion," I connect the dots.

"So, give me the damn keys to my car so we can leave!" the Necromancer shrills, and I find myself reaching for the keys, though I don't want to. But beneath the command and the shrill, the fast-approaching footsteps decide my next move.

Not her.

I grab her arm and, instead of unlocking the door to her mangled car, I click the button to the Roma, pull the door open, and push her into it. She yelps when her head hits the frame, but I keep pushing her rotund body into the passenger seat until she's inside the Roma. The cat meows and purrs against my skin where I'm holding the Necromancer, and I strangely feel comforted by the touch. My frown deepens.

"What are you doing?" the Necromancer whines from inside the sleek vehicle, rubbing her injured temple. She looks ridiculous in the small space, uncomfortable and heavyset. I've rarely had anyone in the car with me other than Tyran and Kali, whenever she's in town, and they're half the Necromancer's size! She shrinks the car around her!

I slam the door on her words, rush to the driver's side, and slip into the seat. With my thumb over the Start/Stop screen, the engine purrs to life. The echo of footsteps climbs up and down the walls of the garage until three dark figures emerge from the stairwell.

League Agents.

When the Black Hearts were dismantled, the League was created. Kind of like the Vampire police, they keep the peace and enforce the rules of the Courts Council. I despise their pretentious existence!

The Necromancer's voice is silenced by fear, and the intensity of her fear pushes against my psyche and chest. It stinks up the car, distracting me. I flip the *manettino* switch to ESC Off mode to turn off the traction control and peel out of the parking spot with the speed of an experienced driver. The tires squeal, smoke encasing the Roma as I pass the two Agents, Rhain and Malik.

Tyran is the third figure, and, for a split second, our eyes meet. His expression, though, is unexpected. While the Agents glare with exposed fangs and ultraviolet firearms, Tyran watches coolly. Not with anger or amusement, but with keen interest.

Even though our eyes barely meet, it's long enough for him to remind me that, even though she's my new Mistress, he will forever be my Sire. And for the first time since Tyran spared a dying man's life of illness and despair, I resent being a servant to anyone.

Chapter 6: The Precision of Timing (Suri)

We're going too fast.

We're going too fast.

I frantically repeat it over and over again in my head like a mantra that might keep us alive. My stomach clenches tightly to my spleen, my fingers habitually tugging at the gloves. The city lights blur through the early-morning traffic, the honking of cars lasting seconds before it dies out, replaced by tires screeching and my own inner screaming that Kilian is going to kill us both!

Well, me, since Kilian is immortal. Then again, bound to me, I suppose he's as mortal as I am if I die.

At one point, I could've sworn I heard police sirens before those, too, were cut off and left behind as an impertinent background noise. When a police cruiser approaches at full speed, nearly colliding with us, a scream is finally ripped out of me, eliciting a cold grin from the Vampire Risen. But then the cruiser slows until it makes a complete stop to watch us pass.

I stare in dejected shock and whisper, "What the hell?"

"Not hell," Kilian replies coolly. "Vampires."

"They're Vampires?"

"No," he pronounces impatiently. "*I* am."

Of course. I should've known that his mesmer could reach further than just his eyes. His memories revealed that his mind and willpower are incredibly strong even though he doesn't use it for good. It's because of his Sire's extensive life. He's much stronger than Kilian, though much less violent and aggressive. He doesn't need to be. He's powerful and cunning.

When the cityscape changes to countryside, I try to relax in the tiny seat, wiggling my hips to find some comfort where there isn't any. Aislynn jumps from my lap into Kilian's, who's as surprised by it as I am. She cuddles up against his midriff and instantly falls asleep. I glare at the treacherous feline with narrowed eyes, especially when Kilian tentatively touches her back and caresses her into a sleepy purr.

I frown childishly and shift in the small seat with growing unease. Yesterday I was a distinguished archivist at a prestigious university and today I'm in way over my head with a very powerful and violent Vampire as my Risen, his even more powerful and shrewd Sire following us, and a tiny car that makes me look like a hippo!

Now I've gotten myself stuck in the middle of the supernatural world I've spent my entire life avoiding at any cost and bringing it all to Nana's doorstep in the Bayou, putting her at risk as well. Even though it's only a couple of hours away, I must find a way to make the trip longer, even for this tiny, speedy car and the brooding Vampire who drives it.

I blink away the anxiety crawling up my throat and turn my attention to Kilian's profile. Despite his height, he looks almost regal in the expensive car, the red interior glowing in the low-lit blue screens and deeply tinted windows. My eyes travel up from his poisonous lips to his fine nose and over his furrowed forehead.

Though he broods, he isn't frowning, which is a first for me. He may not be frowning, but he's still tense and terse, which adds to my worry. I'm not afraid that he'll hurt me, because he can't. But I don't doubt he'll leverage Nana against me and then kill us both when the bond is broken.

If the bond can be broken.

"Stop staring," he growls, startling me and ruining the moment. He's frowning again, so I turn away, brooding in my own thoughts. How stupid could I have been to have suggested that the bond could be broken? I've never heard Nana mention ways a Master-Risen bond could be broken, but I'm hoping it's because the topic simply never came up.

"Stop *staring* at me," Kilian repeats with annoyance, and I jump in the tight space, banging my head on the low ceiling. I didn't even realize I'd glanced in his direction. I shift my body again, my hips awkwardly spilling over the sides of the seat.

"Ugh!" I complain with annoyance. "Why is this car so small?"

Kilian's eyebrow goes up when he glances at me and tilts his head, glances at the comfort of his own body as it fits perfectly in the confines of the vehicle, then back at me. I frown because I can easily interpret his expression: I'm too fat for the sports car.

I sit completely still, my heart beating with indignation. I force myself *not* to be ashamed of my weight, angry at my stupidity for having saved the life of a soulless Vampire who hadn't been trying to save me like I'd thought and overwhelmed by the results.

After several minutes of mental self-deprecation and physical discomfort, I silence the negativity and remind myself of the reason I unashamedly chose to be overweight. I had to do it in order to generate enough energy to use the three gifts in case I needed all three. I need enough calories to distribute energy evenly throughout my body, mostly for Seeing and Blinking, since I use the skill most often. I'm damn good at both *because* I have enough energy for them. I have enough energy *because* my body stores it in fat cells, not in muscle.

I shift my body again, trying to find a less awkward position where the edges of the seat don't cut into my outer thighs and hips and my self-consciousness won't draw any more ugly attention from the moody driver. Even so, I glance at Kilian with annoyance, his eyes fixed on the road, and my frown turns ugly. His perfect Vampire body may fit in tiny cars, but my ass doesn't!

Kilian grumbles, "Stop that!"

"I can't! I'm uncomfortable!" I snap back, cutting him a glance. "The seats are too small and I'm too…" I stumble for an appropriate word that will describe my weight without openly shaming me. Instead, the words clomp out of my head and my cheeks inflame with irritation.

I'm still trying to find a comparable word when Kilian states, "Uncomfortable. Yes, you've made that very obvious." I'm taken aback by his unexpected response. I thought he would fill in the blank with offensive comments.

His long arm reaches the center flat screen between us, taps several times, and surprises me when the seat shifts beneath me, making it wide enough for me to finally sit comfortably. He glances at me, his gray eyes like moving mercury when I sigh in relief. I smile and am about to say *Thank You* when he frowns and turns away. I bite my lip and swallow my gratitude.

"How do you know where we're going?" I ask, my eyes blinking slowly. Now that I'm more comfortable, my exhaustion sits heavily on my lids, and I force them to stay open. Even though Kilian's mesmer knocked me out, his childhood memories of Salem plagued my sleep.

"I'm taking us to a safehouse," he reveals. "One only Tyran and I know about."

Worry creases my forehead because I know that Kilian's relationship with me is nowhere near his relationship with Tyran. While Kilian must obey me and follow the Code, Tyran doesn't, and Tyran is cunning enough to just follow from a distance.

"Won't Tyran follow us?"

"Yes, but he won't come for you yet." His words do not comfort me at all.

"How do you know?" I insist, and he turns on me impatiently.

"Because I know him better than you do. You may have my memories and feelings, but you don't know him. You can only experience my side of him. Not his."

I turn away when he does, frowning, because he is *so* wrong about how I know Tyran. I don't distrust Tyran because he's Kilian's best friend who has protected him, trained him, saved him countless times in battle and missions, and loves him as a brother. I don't trust him because of the *ways* he's done all those things. His cunning and ambition are more dangerous than his fangs and claws. I don't share my perspective with Kilian, though, and instead, command, "Pull over now and release me."

Kilian's scowl is so deep the sharp edges of his cheeks glint like razor blades. The only evidence that my order has had some minor effect is that the car slows down to the speed limit and remains there.

"Dammit, why won't you obey my commands?"

"Because I'm not human," he growls.

"But you're my Risen!" I yell back and, even though the heat emerging from his anger is palpable, he doesn't answer. "You could hate it as much as I do, but there's still the Code."

"Not killing you is the only one I'm forced to follow."

My eyes widen in indignation, and I order, "Release me, Risen! Release me now!" He hits the brakes so hard my upper body is violently thrown forward. The seatbelt is the only reason my brains aren't splattered all over the dashboard.

As soon as my heart stops banging against my chest, I turn to Kilian with the intention of giving him a piece of my mind, but the intense way his marble black orbs stare traps my tongue on the insult. Because there's more than just his angry Vampire eyes. He's breathing erratically and sweating, fighting the command with the willpower that has worked for him for centuries.

His grip on the wheel is so tight it's denting slightly.

I quickly glance at his lap, worried by the hand wrapped around Aislynn. He'd held her when he'd hit the brakes so she wouldn't be splattered all over the car's display, but his hold on her is gentle.

Before the order fades in his mind, I peer out at the rising sun along a hilly horizon and try to open the door. The car is so damn fancy that I can't even figure out how it opens. When I find the button—not a handle! —I frantically throw the door open. The cool breeze slaps my face while Kilian hisses at the sunlight slipping into the interior darkness. I quickly step out and whistle for Aislynn to follow, but don't dare look at Kilian's face, afraid of what I'll see while I coax my cat to come to me.

"You treacherous feline," I chastise when Aislynn refuses to leave Kilian. I lift my eyes to his and instantly regret it because, though they're still angry, they're a silvery gray. Apparently, it's his human side that I'm beginning to fear the most.

"You won't go far," he says self-assuredly, slowly petting Aislynn to prove a point. "Much less without your cat." Aislynn purrs in agreement, and I frown at both.

"Don't look for me, Kilian, or you'll force me to kill you."

Strangely, the threat of setting Kilian on fire until he's nothing but cinders and ash bothers me, and I draw my brows at my reaction. While I have a deep attachment to the traitorous cat, I'd always attributed it to having owned her for as long as I can remember.

Maybe there's more to our relationship than that. Maybe that's why I'm unhappy with the idea of killing Kilian. But I don't have time to dwell on the intricacies of Master and Risen personal relationships right now.

"Tyran will find you even if you order me not to," Kilian warns, and I don't doubt the Sire will try to find me. But he won't. With Nana's help, I'll leave the most minimal supernatural traces, especially because I'm not the only one who leaves supernatural traces behind.

"I'll always know where you are," Kilian adds, stilling my thoughts. "The taste of your blood binds you to me."

Dammit, he's right!

He'd forced a Blood Bond when he'd tasted my blood and will forever find me, no matter where I go or for how long I run. But the archives of Vampire legends indicate that the further the range, the dimmer the ability. It'll always be present, unless I take a rocket to outer space like one of those billionaire tourists to Mars. But it'll take Kilian longer to find me, especially if I keep moving, which I intend to do.

I stare at his haughty eyes for long seconds, the furrow along his brow, the grimace of his mouth, wishing that he'd never been sent to terminate me. Wishing the Gargoyles hadn't been following him. Wishing I'd not made the mistake of thinking they'd been following me. Wishing I'd never touched him with my bare hand and saved his life, believing he was saving mine.

Wishing this sexy-as-sin man was attracted to me and would search for me with all his being because of love instead of obsessive duty. Instead, he despised me.

"I'm sorry," I whisper genuinely, blink quickly, and slam the door in his face, leaving my cat and the Risen who'd seduced her to his dark side.

I quickly glance around, trying to gauge my bearings. The road is surrounded by fields of green grass and several groves of trees. There's nothing else, though. No house. No gas station. Not even a barn. I have no idea where I am, and I scold myself at my lack of preplanning. Again!

I sigh heavily because I only have one option and, while I hate to show Kilian the extent of my gift, I have no choice. I jog to the front of the car, so it won't distort the image that I need to know where I am and where I need to go. Making sure there aren't any cars coming, I take a breath and nervously remove one of my gloves.

I instantly feel Kilian's eyes on me, as if the removal of my gloves brought him closer to me. It's unnerving. It's exciting.

I ignore the sudden guilt of having to leave him—and Aislynn—behind and, with my heart in my mouth and my breath just behind it, I lower my hand to the asphalt, fingers splayed, and touch it.

Flashing images slam against my mind with more force than I'd expected, robbing me of breath and balance. Just like with Kilian, my mind absorbs all the road's history, from its birth as an animal crossing to a gravel path and then asphalt. But, unlike Kilian, the land itself leaves a mark on my mind, along with the experiences of every animal, human, supernatural, and vehicle that has ever crossed its path.

Memories are like shards of glass cutting into sections of my mind that insert themselves as part of my experience. I rarely touch inanimate objects simply to seek information, except for the ancient manuscripts in the university archives. Even so, it's only when I've expended all other forms of research or to confirm it.

I should've known that touching the road would be too much. I should've never touched it because the more transited the object, the more overload of experiences assaults me.

For a moment, where time stretches slowly between the road and my hand, I lose all sense of sight, sound, and touch, like I'm stuck inside a sensory vacuum, depriving me of anything outside my mind and body, even though my eyes are still open. Pain like lightning cuts through me in a shaft of history and memory. I yank my hand back with a cry and collapse, keeping my exposed hand off the road and avoiding more flashes. My head pounds with the same cadence of each pump of my heart, the dim sunrise stabbing at it mercilessly.

There are 3,482 animal carcasses buried beneath the road in a radius of one mile. Three-hundred-twelve male bodies, one-hundred-eighty-four females, and sixty-eight children are buried, their bones clawing at my essence, a desperate tug in my chest for renewed life. I whimper with abject sorrow for their deaths, my soul wanting to reach out to each one and give it another chance.

I fist my hands and resist the desperate need to animate! I'm on Highway 52, but it's not a direct route to the Bayou, just a side road that runs alongside a major highway I'd have to take further south from here.

Dammit! Five-hundred-and-sixty-four corpses begging for my gift and I'm nowhere near where I need to be!

A large shadow blocks the sun briefly and I exhale for the momentary reprieve, but the shade also intensifies my exhaustion, heightens the demand to give life. It takes me precious seconds to realize that the shadow is a body. Too late does Kilian's voice break through the vacuum of misery and silence when he whispers my name, picks me up in his arms, and returns me to the car as if I weighed nothing. Extremely weakened by my lack of sleep, fatigue, and supernatural gifts, my head reluctantly leans against his chest. He carefully places me in the vehicle's passenger seat, mumbling something in another language. I sigh in relief when the car door closes and sequesters me in darkness.

No wonder Kilian drives this car!

He returns to the driver's seat, presses a button instead of turning an ignition or grabbing a stick shift, and speeds off. We're both silent, and I side-eye him, guilt crawling up my throat that his body is smoking from having been exposed to the sun to rescue me. I close my eyes when Aislynn perches herself on my lap, meowing her concern for me.

But the heat from Kilian's anger reminds me he's no hero rescuing a damsel in distress. He's a Vampire, a killer seeking escape from servitude to then deliver me to the highest supernatural bidder. The darkness behind my eyes pulls me in deeper, until the fist in my chest loosens up, and everything around me slows to a background crawl.

Chapter 7: A Midnight Stop (Suri)

A tall boy stood on a balcony overlooking the breaking shores outside his home. He was eight and healthy, despite the malaria outbreak among the plebeians that he only heard about from the servants. His hands were clasped behind his back, deep in thought for a boy so young.

But his thoughts were not on the malady of the proletariat. It was his younger sister, Annette, who'd been sick with an ailment very different from malaria. For the past weeks, she'd lost interest in playing, no longer laughing or crying. She was so thin her clothes hung on her small body, her golden hair losing its luster, and her gray eyes sunken in its sockets.

Consumption.

That was what the servants whispered in the halls of the family mansion. The boy wasn't clear about what it meant, but that was what they were saying Annette was suffering from.

At the sound of her coughing in the bedroom behind him, the boy frowned, his hands tightening into fists. Annette was two years younger than him and often a nuisance. But she was his sister, his only sibling and, with Mama dead, she was his only family.

Papa didn't count as family anymore.

He spent most of his time traveling, often leaving the children with the servants, especially after Mama died from the same illness that ailed Annette. Papa hadn't returned from his latest trip, even though the servants had made him aware of her illness. But the boy knew he was not returning, not until Annette died, and he hated Papa for it.

His frown darkened into a scowl, his chest pounding, the sound of his anger pumping in his ears like his quickening pulse. Annette was all he had left, and he would lose her like he'd lost their mother. His father simply abandoned her, too, when she'd become ill. Annette had only been four years old, leaving him as the "man of the household while I'm gone away."

At the time, the boy had believed it to be an honor. But then Mama died, and Papa returned months later, older and distant, only to leave again and spend more time away than at home. The boy and Annette became accustomed to not having him around because they had each other. But Annette had been sick for a couple of weeks now, and the boy held no hope for her recovery. He'd already been witness to his mother's illness.

Annette's coughing pierced his thoughts, and the fist in his chest only tightened. The boy turned around, bright gray eyes gazing into the candlelit room, with fear and determination. He would not become his father and turn away from Annette's suffering. Unlike Mama, she would not die alone.

Standing taller than his age, the boy stepped into the bedroom to keep his sister company, Salem shuffling behind him with a wanton purr.

"Suri."

The sound of my name is wrapped inside a dark voice like silk.

"Mm?" I mutter, blinking my eyes open. I turn my head toward the voice. The same gray eyes from my dream meet mine.

The boy.

Kilian.

"What was that about?" he demands angrily, throwing my gloves at me. Startled by his aggression, I shift uneasily in the seat. I tug the gloves back on, struggling to connect his question to the dream. He's not referring to the dream, but to the psychometry on the road. I turn my gaze away, unwilling to reveal any more of my skills to the Vampire whose memories have become my dreams.

"If you wanted to know the road we were on, you should've asked and not used your gifts!" he chastises impatiently.

When I still don't reply, he growls angrily, "Why were you so weak? Your eyes rolled back, and you collapsed. In the sunlight! I could've been pulverized, and you could've died!"

"Oh, God forbid I die and take you with me," I mutter sarcastically.

"God has nothing to do with this!" he sneers, and I swallow another snarky remark because I'm still too tired and he's clearly very upset. I wouldn't have died, anyway. At least, I don't think I can from Psychometry. I've been touching ancient and occult scrolls for years now and haven't died and, though there have been several times when I'd blacked out, I've never needed to stay long at the hospital.

It's the Necromancy that affects me more. But how to explain the way corpses call to me wherever they're buried, demanding a second chance at life? The way Nana had to train me to push away the strong wrenching in my chest to give life to the dead because it was a powerful and overwhelming force. The way I avoid cemeteries because I sob in grief and guilt when I reject the pull. Kilian thinks being a Seer is what drains me when, in fact, it's the very gift that gave him life that breaks my body and soul.

We don't speak when one highway turns into another that spills into yet another until my stomach rumbles like an old man complaining. Despite being in and out of sleep during the ride, nightmarish snippets of Kilian's memories wake me with a shudder each time, and rest eludes me. Starved and badly needing to pee, I jiggle in the cushioned seat, tugging my gloves with anxiety.

After frowning and grimacing every time my stomach clenches loudly with hunger, Kilian finally pulls into a small diner and parks furthest from the entrance.

"Keep your gloves on," he orders, and I frown. Does he think I'm dumb enough to walk around other people without coverings? One mishap and he thinks I'm irresponsible!

"If you remove them for anything without telling me first, I will…"

Rudely interrupting him, I say, "You do *not* order me around, Kilian." His expression darkens at the mention of his name, but he continues, undaunted by my threat.

"Did you use your Psychometry gift on the road?" I don't reply, even when he leans too close to my neck. I clench my jaw and force myself not to move, though a tremulous breath escapes me.

"Don't lie," he warns, and I shiver, knowing that Vampires are masters at scenting emotions, but blood-bound Vampires can also scent lies.

"I did," I admit quietly. "But I'm not going to tell you more."

Dammit, he's hungry! His eyes turn red again, though the pupil is wider than it had been when I first met him.

"You've told me enough." *Hardly.* It's not memory and experience he should fear for me. It's death and decay. I squeal when he grabs me by the neck and pulls me close, inhaling deeply. Tears spring to my eyes, even though I know he won't kill me. Threat of what his fangs can do scares the hell out of me, anyway.

I scream, though, when Kilian sinks his fangs into my skin. He pulls out quickly, licking the dripping blood from my neck before it spreads. Despite the warmth of his tongue as it laps up my blood, licking it until it heals, there's a different kind of pain that hurts more. It's the realization that my Risen has hurt me.

When I was eleven, Aislinn scratched my thigh, trying to climb up to my lap. While the scratch didn't even bleed, I pushed her off me and ignored her for the rest of the day, emotionally hurt that she'd physically hurt me. Not even Nana's consolations softened the pain. It was only when Aislinn whined for hours outside my bedroom door until I let her in.

Kilian has hurt me in the same way. The physical scar is gone, but the emotional one will last much longer. He pulls away, my blood staining his lips, making me nauseous. His very-pink tongue slowly slips out to lick the crimson droplets, and he closes his eyes, groaning. When he opens them, they're a bright silver instead of blood red. His hand still holds the back of my neck, the pull of his mesmer drawing me, seductive and enticing. I quickly close my eyes, breathing heavily, before I lose myself in them.

"Two can play at that game, Mistress," he whispers, his coppery breath fanning my lips. I whimper when his moist tongue licks my cheek so slowly, I'm sure I'll pass out from fear. Kilian groans again and adds with a growly tremor, "It's been a while since I've tasted fresh tears and enjoyed it like this."

"Get off of me," I order slowly, in a tremulous croak, opening my eyes so that he knows it's an order. Kilian's long tongue freezes over his lower lip, his eyes narrowing with silent refusal. But he gradually leans away.

Up close like this, his eyes aren't just a solid gray, but a mix of different shades of gray, lined by a thin dark blue ring, blending into the gray. They're beautiful. Spellbinding. Dangerous.

I'm startled when Kilian presses a button on the dashboard that moves my seat back. He opens the glove compartment, pulls out a wad of cash, and throws twenty dollars on my lap. I clasp the right side of my lower lip between my teeth and suck silently.

"Go eat," he orders as if he were *my* Master. I frown, but he continues. "You have twenty minutes. If you are late, I drain the blood of every person who leaves before you do until you come out."

I stare wide-eyed and shocked by the threat. Flashbacks of his memories in my dreams indicate he is more than capable of such a massacre. Frightened, I grab the money and rush out of the car when the nauseating smell of my blood adds to the violent memories of his past.

I walk into the cool night, darkness barely filtering through the artificial light of headlights and parking-lot lampposts. I measure my steps, not wanting to attract any attention and careful not to look like a crazy woman running from a Vampire. I don't doubt Kilian will kill anyone who might accost me with concern.

I take a deep breath as the grubby glass doors come into view, wipe the sweat from my brow, and step into the most hackneyed diner I've ever seen. The place smells of greasy burgers and French fries; the booths are a fading red, and the patrons are as transient as the midwestern wind. I stand idly by the door, fumbling with my gloved fingers, until a tall, skinny waitress with a waist the size of my wrist and a bust spilling over her white shirt approaches with a customary smile.

"Sit anywhere you like, sweetie," she invites. "Someone'll be right with you." I sit at the counter nearest the door, not wanting to waste any time getting back to the car when my time is up.

"Whatcha want, honey?" the waitress behind the counter asks. She's the opposite of the hostess. Heavyset with blue eyes, like bleached jeans, and wrinkles as old as the booths. I feel better with her! I place my order and nervously glance behind me at the red car that stood out like a sore thumb amidst a sea of dull sedans, pickup trucks, and 18-wheelers. But the beauty outside can't hide the death and danger that lurks within the tinted windows. The waitress speaks again, and I turn to face her.

"Do you want any sides with that?" she repeats with an impatient roll of her eyes as she pointedly glances at the other patrons at the counter.

"No, thank you, and please hurry. I'm in a rush." Her mouth collapses at both ends and she sighs heavily.

"Everyone here is." She pours coffee into a bland mug, then turns to relay the order to the cook.

My hands shake as I pour sugar into the mug, slowly adding three small containers of half-and-half, as I've done since I started drinking coffee. I stare into the mug's wide opening; the cream rising from the bottom of the blackness, billows of white and tan slowly spreading across the surface of the darker coffee in engrossing swirls.

Mama had once said that our ancestor gypsies would read gorgers their futures by interpreting the grains of tea at the bottom of their teacups. Nana had laughed at her and said only desperate fools would trust tea residue to reveal their futures. Her eyes had met mine, suddenly looking so young and full of mischief that the hairs along my forearms tingled, and said, "No one drinks tea anymore. The augurs are hidden in the creamers." She'd cackled like a madwoman when Mama groaned, and I smiled warmly at both women.

I stare at the creamer as it rises and dilutes, not to tell my future, which I'd rather *not* know, but to calm my nerves.

"If you stare that intently, will it foretell the future?"

I startle at the question, nearly slipping off the stool, and lift my eyes to the patron beside me. He's a large, bulky Black man with dark eyes the color of coal and a clean-shaven head. His features are rough and bold, but a friendly smirk hangs from his lips despite the mug of coffee looking too small in his large hand. He takes a sip and motions to my coffee with a nod.

"Your coffee. My grandmother used to say she could read the future based on the coffee grains at the bottom of the mug." I almost roll my eyes like Nana would. "You may be doing the opposite there." I glance at the coffee whose cream has already blended enough with the coffee to lose its calming effect, no thanks to Mr. Nosy beside me.

I look up sheepishly at the stranger and say, "Nothing to see in the coffee but a much-needed kick to get me on my way."

"And which way is that?" he asks curiously. I frown at his intrusive question and am about to tell him where *he* should go when he chuckles and pulls out his hand, introducing himself.

"Korday." I glance at it, then back at his dark, friendly eyes, and shake his hand.

"Su… Sarah," I offer, since my name has already gotten me in trouble, then pull my hand away.

"Gloves, huh?" I shrug.

"What brings you to this particular diner on this particular day, Korday?"

He peers at me as if trying to understand the intention of my question, then smirks and says, "The fortune-telling coffee?"

A giggle escapes me, and I shake my head in embarrassment, quickly glancing behind me again, afraid Kilian might misinterpret whatever this nice guy is doing. When my meal arrives, I eat it quickly and in silence, expertly making sure not to get my gloves stained, and avoid looking at the stranger beside me who hasn't ordered anything else.

In the years I've learned to hide from the supernatural, I've kept friendships at arm's length. For one, I can't tell one supernatural from another. While they can scent each other and have other ways to identify one race from the next, I have no such abilities. To befriend a supernatural is as dangerous as friending a wild animal and expecting it not to devour me when it's hungry.

To friend a human, though, is even more dangerous because it means inevitably exposing that person to the supernatural world. I may be human, but the supernatural gifts isolate me from the human *and* the supernatural worlds, stuck somewhere in no-man's land. But I've gotten used to living in between the two worlds and belonging to neither and have learned that relationships need to be fleeting and superficial before suspicions are made and questions asked.

Losing track of time, I quickly glance around the diner for a clock and jump when Korday's deep voice announces, "It's almost midnight." I nod and try to smile, but the time isn't exactly what I need.

"How long have I been sitting here?"

Korday stares at me, his eyes strangely intent, before he lifts the mug to his lips and sips his coffee while I watch impatiently. "I've been sitting here for about ten minutes. You arrived earlier than I did." He shrugs.

Okay. That means I have enough time to pay for my meal, use the bathroom, and run back to the car without Kilian getting involved.

"Thank you," I hear myself say and debate whether I should take the time to pee or just run out before my time is up. Kilian doesn't strike me like the kind of guy who'll make another pit stop any time soon, so I make time!

I throw Kilian's twenty-dollar bill on the counter and head straight for the bathroom, glancing out the window for signs of Kilian. The flashy car is still parked where I'd left it, but my heart thumps fearfully. I don't know what I'm anticipating might happen, since my gifts never really explain themselves to me, but expectation crackles the air around me.

When I turn my attention away from the window, I nearly collide into a waitress and slow down before I make a scene that'll take more than the three minutes I intend to be in the bathroom. I shuffle in more discreetly and take care of my needs.

After washing my hands and throwing some water on my face, I dare a glance in the mirror and am surprised I don't look worse. Sure, my dark hair is a mess, I have black circles under my eyes, and my breath smells like coffee. But I don't look worse than an overworked waitress who works a second job.

I run out of the bathroom because there's no time to waste trying to touch up the mess on my head and maneuver my way through the growing crowd to the front door. I take another peek at the window and stop dead in my tracks, fear crashing into me from behind. The car isn't there, the gaudy red gone from the dark parking lot. My breath catches in my throat and my heart goes into overdrive.

I practically run outside before a now-familiar voice chastises, "Whoa," as I collide into Korday's expansive back.

"Sorry," I squeak and try to push past him because he's blocking the doorway. "Move. Move, please!"

"Easy," he grumbles and moves into the space where neon lights blare a shoddy welcome, one letter blinking every several seconds. I squint, anxiously looking for Kilian or the car. My stomach drops when I don't see either, because I'm sure Kilian didn't just abandon me. I'd love to think he finally obeyed my order and left. But it's more likely my timing isn't exactly his, and he thinks I'm late, lurking somewhere to kill the first person out of the diner.

I turn to Korday, wide-eyed and scared for him, because *he's* the first one who'd come out before me! "Are you okay?" he asks with genuine concern.

"Go back inside," I suggest frantically, pushing him back. Or, at least, trying to. He doesn't budge an inch despite my effort.

But it's too late. I freeze when I sense Kilian's presence behind me, like I've sprouted dark wings. The weight of his cold hand on my shoulder makes me shiver with staggering fear, crippling me. I can't turn around, frozen in place and afraid to face the killer who's incapable of killing me but won't hesitate to hurt me. And there's nothing holding him back from killing because of me.

"How?" Korday says with incredulity as I stare in fear. But his eyes aren't fixed on me. He's glaring over my head, the skin of his face rippling like wet cement, changing from chocolate brown to ashen gray and back. The top of his head stretches into two small

82

horns that disappear seconds later, only to peek out again. The neon lights add to his macabre transformation.

"You're a Gargoyle," I mutter, realization hitting me like a ton of bricks.

His eyes, dark as night, penetrate through me when he asks in an accusatory tone, "You *saved* him?"

"I…" I begin, but what could I say? He's right. I extended the life of the Vampire being hunted and nearly killed by Gargoyles. There's no explanation that will justify the voluntary saving of a Vampire's undead life.

"Abomination," Korday spats at Kilian with judgmental eyes and a disgusted sneer. Guilt kicks me in the chest that I'd spared the life of a Vampire who isn't worth saving. When Korday's bulky form suddenly pulls away from me with disorienting force, I stifle a scream because *he* isn't the one moving.

I am!

With unnatural speed, Kilian swivels me behind him, protecting me from the threat of the Gargoyle, even though Korday's violence isn't against me. I'd be grateful if Kilian were doing it sincerely, but he's only following his Risen instinct.

Korday says something in another language, not Esperanto. I strain to listen because languages are my forte. It's Latin! His voice, though, is freakishly deeper, more threatening, like the collision of boulders. Kilian responds in the same language, his voice like sharp steel. When Korday addresses me, I snap my eyes to his and shiver against Kilian's back. There's no anger or violence in Korday's eyes. Just a deep abyss of blackness.

"You can come with me," he offers in English. "I'm not alone, and we can subdue this abomination. We know what you are and can offer protection from him and... from others of his kind."

Knows what I am? Does he mean as an Animator, or a Ternion?

Kilian hisses, his body shaking with anger when he warns, "You will *not* take her without bloodshed." Korday laughs, the thunderous sound like imminent violence sending a shiver up my spine. Kilian tenses in response.

"You cannot kill three of us on your own," Korday scoffs. The heat from Kilian's body goes up by degrees, and my heart smashes against my chest when he slowly turns his head toward a nosy onlooker.

The skinny guy in his forty's watches behind thick, black-rimmed glasses, curious about the unfolding drama outside the diner. He shrieks when Kilian grabs him by the face and smashes his head against the diner's glass door with a loud crash. Glass splinters and shatters, but I only hear the thumping pop of the man's head, blood and brains splattering across the stucco. The man crumbles to the ground, and my scream joins those of other witnesses to the unnatural violence.

Screams erupt around me, humans running from the scene of violence. I drop my eyes as a thick plume of black smoke gathers at my feet, billowing upward. It speedily wraps itself around Kilian legs, covering us in thick darkness. I barely have time to register what's happening, much less heed Korday's offer.

His black unnatural eyes beckon for me and I nod in desperation, reaching out to him from around Kilian's frame. But Kilian grabs my hand in his, wrapping his longer fingers between my stubby ones. A long blade materializes in Korday's hand, because his jeans are too fitting to hide a blade that large, and he only wears a Patriots T-shirt across his wide chest. By the time he advances on Kilian, the inky cloud has completely engulfed us and, too late, do I realize the smoke isn't black smoke from a fire.

It's crimson mist!

Much like cephalopod ink from octopi and squid, crimson mist is a Vampire's defense mechanism when feeling threatened. Unlike octopi and squid that take advantage of the distraction to swim away, a Vampire can disappear through teleportation. When the ground drops from under my feet, another scream is stifled by loss of breath, the air too thin to remain conscious.

Chapter 8: The Possessed Vampire (Suri)

A sickly thin body laid motionless on a hospital bed. The room was shaded by dark curtains blocking a deeper darkness that lurked dangerously close outside. The cadaver was more bones than skin, pulled back so tightly the nurses that attended him were unnerved the young man still clung to life. But they remained in service in exchange for the coin his wealth provided.

The young man knew their only fealty was to his money and that, if it ever dried out, they'd leave him to die in the opulent hospital afforded only to the most prestigious families of wealth and power. They were already showing hints of his suspicion and the money hadn't even run out. But neither had his final breath.

A familiar voice chatted away outside his suite, but Kilian was too weak to even smile. Even so, he recognized the unmistakable baritone voice, the rich laughter, and the glimmer of hope that he wasn't going to die alone. After all, his newfound friend had visited him several times in the last several weeks since his illness became terminal.

The voice drew near, each word laced with laughter and youthful life, while the dying man's youth had already withered away. When the door opened, Kilian couldn't even turn his head to greet his friend.

"Ah, Mr. Willingham," the man spoke jovially, in a heavily accented voice, Irish or Scottish. "Good to see you awake. I've come

about that proposition we'd spoken of last week." Kilian blinked in acknowledgment and the other man, blonde hair too long to be an aristocrat and green eyes sparkling with life, softly closed the door. Kilian envied his youthful glow and even the man's kindness. The friend didn't have to keep returning to visit a dying man, but he'd come once a week with news of the world and the same offer every time.

"Come, end this life at my mansion in the hills, and start a new one with me."

The same offer, week after week, as Kilian's body deteriorated into nothing but skin and bones. His mind remained sharp, though, which Kilian resented the most because he'd rather be losing his mind along with the rest of him than live trapped in a body that was dying slowly.

"Still refusing laudanum, I see," the vital friend commented, not unkindly. Kilian made a grunting sound that elicited a chuckle from his friend. "Good for you, Mr. Willingham. A man of your inner strength should no longer dwell in a dwindling body too small for your spirit. Will you come then?"

The man leaned over Kilian, but the decadent smell of death clung to Kilian even before it had claimed him, shaming him. It didn't seem to bother his friend, though, who pressed in closer and repeated his offer in a slow, melodic tone. He'd done it before, his soothing baritone voice comforting Kilian.

Even so, each time the friend made his offer, Kilian politely declined, to which the friend would nod solemnly and admit, "Your spirit is strong, my friend. You deserve another life."

To live his last days of shame and utter weakness was deplorable in a hospital setting, much worse among the living. But he'd begun to see the way the nurses and staff seemed too eager for his death. Careless in their ministrations with him. Remiss to bathe him. Sometimes, even eating the food meant to strengthen him rather than feed it to him. If Kilian didn't die from his illness, he would certainly die from their neglect.

He managed a small nod to his friend, whose pinkish lips stretched into a genuine smile. But there was something unnatural in his green eyes. Something predatory. The kindly eyes that had brought comfort during the last few weeks now filled with emotionless blackness, completely concealing the whites.

Behind the smile, glistening elongated fangs dripped with thick saliva when the young friend cajoled, "Don't worry, Kilian Willingham. Dubhshláin O'Catháin, ancient Celt, son of the wilds, will take care of you." He rushed to Kilian's neck with unnatural speed and sank the fangs into what little muscle remained. Kilian's mouth fell open in a silent scream no one would have heard, even if they tried.

A last, warm tear fell down the side of Kilian's cheek, life finally releasing its hold on him, only to be violently wrenched back by a different form of virus. But also, by something far more menacing.

Something far deadlier than death itself.

I wake with a sob jammed in my throat, my hand covering my neck where Tyran had bitten Kilian. The pain of memory is as real as that of psychometry. My heart beats erratically, matching my breath, tears streaming down my cheeks as flashes of death and Turning linger behind my eyes.

Another one of his memories slipped into my dreams and I'm caught unaware of the effect it has on me. As Kilian's Mistress, I knew I'd have some control over him and would see and feel his experiences at the moment of touch. But I hadn't considered dreaming his memories, with all the feelings and emotions connected with them as a Seer.

I wipe the tears and take a steadying breath, nervously peering into the enveloping darkness. I'm no longer in the car or outside a diner watching a Gargoyle challenge a Vampire. I'm lying on a massive four-poster bed surrounded by red silk curtains. Past the silk, sunlight haloes thick curtains that block two windows along the left wall. Elaborate furniture adorns the loft, dominated by the bed and an unlit fireplace so big two Santas could fit through it!

I shift to get off the bed and nearly scream when I fall onto the body of a corpse! I scurry away on hand and butt, staring at it, and my heart clenches when I realize it's not a corpse. I would've known it was there before I'd even woken. A sob breaks through when I recognize that it's the same emaciated form of the Kilian from my dream!

The wrinkled pages of an ancient Romanian tome flash through my mind, one that asserts that, when Vampires sleep, they take their true form. But I had always understood it to mean the Vampire form, with fangs and monstrous features, though Kilian has always just looked hot and sexy. I *definitely* hadn't expected that Kilian's true form would be him on his deathbed!

His face is deeply grooved, his closed eyes sunken inside the bottomless pits of his face. Cheek bones poke out like steep mountain ranges connecting a bald skull to his sharp jawbones. His

89

nose is thin and upturned over a small dry mouth stamped by pale, chapped lips, slightly parted.

I drop my head and weep in silence. Not so much for the sickly man Kilian had once been, no longer able to refuse the offer Tyran had made him. These tears were for my mother, who'd died of cancer and appeared the same way. Unlike Mama, Kilian had replaced a life of illness and death with one of blood and violence. While I pity the man Kilian had been, whose suffering I know through Mama's experience and his memories, I can't condone the Vampire he's become.

The nosy bystander's smashed-in head flares in my mind, and I blink the horrible image away, repressing the guilt of having been the cause of it. I nearly scream when soft fur grazes my hand and Aislynn purrs against me. I let out a silent sigh of relief and gently run my hand over her back, reminding myself that she will protect me, even if Kilian doesn't know how yet.

At least, I hope the treacherous little beast will protect me from him!

Slowly, I scoot away from Kilian, careful not to tilt the bed too much to not wake him. Luckily, the mattress is firm enough to not shake the dead. Aislynn watches me with wise, yellow eyes, but doesn't move from Kilian's side. I motion for her to come and nod encouragingly. She just stares. I frown, knowing she's dissing me for him. Again.

I turn to flip my legs over the side and lose my balance on a step I hadn't seen leading to the rugged floor. As a reflex so common among the fat and clumsy, I reach out to break my fall and grab onto the silk sheet wrapped around the four posters. The humiliating ripping sound breaks the silence and, to my shameful horror, the even louder thump of my body hitting the floor wakes Kilian.

"There are precisely thirteen Necromancers in the world at any given time," Kilian snarls, and I jump to my feet at the cold tone that literally drops degrees in the room. "No more and no less, and I'm tethered to the clumsiest one."

His words sting more than they should as I pick myself off the floor and shoot back, "There are precisely thirteen Vampire Courts in every major city around the world that every Vampire belongs to, no more and no less, hence keeping a delicate balance of power monitored closely by the Vampire Courts Council, and I'm tethered to the meanest Vampire who belongs to none."

His silver eyes narrow in a glare that reflects a nonexistent light since nothing is illuminated in the room. But his lip tugs in a wry smile that chokes my breath with fear. I don't know what's outside of this loft, but I'd rather take my chances that we're *not* at another Vampire Court, since it would be counterproductive to escape from one and hide in another.

In a sudden move, I race to the door, but two barriers instantly block my progress. First, I've never been fast, and my body weight slows me down considerably. Second, Kilian is already at the door before I can take three steps; his hands clenched into fists. My breath comes in spurts, and I quickly move left of him, but he follows my movements so precisely it unnerves me. I swallow hard, then move to the right, but he echoes my movements, stopping me in my tracks.

I stand completely still and so does he, his eyes dark and his fleshy lips slanted in a wolfish grin. I'm not faster or stronger, or even smarter than him. But I *am* his Mistress.

I take a deep breath, square my shoulders, and turn my back on him. The move is ballsy, not because he can attack me without my even seeing him, but because it's my silent reminder that I don't need to be afraid of him, robbing him of his control over my fear. He's my Risen and can't kill me, no matter how much he hates me.

I am fully aware, though, that it can also backfire because he's already bitten me twice without killing me and can easily do it again regardless of whether I'm his Mistress or not. I take measured steps toward the fireplace, ignoring the way the hairs on my nape stand on end, my primitive brain igniting the feeling of being stalked. I replace it with the confident truth that he is *my* Risen and *I* have the power over him to keep me alive.

When I reach the fireplace, I quickly busy myself trying to figure out how to light a fire, even though I don't know anything about fireplaces or hearths. I just need a distraction from Kilian's threatening intensity. It's like he suffocates all the air and heat in the room. I find the firewood rack, pick up a manageable log, and place it in the hearth, followed by three more. I jump back with a squeak when the fire roars to life without even having added kindling. I turn in time to find Kilian standing beside me, a flame of fire dancing in the palm of his hand.

"Pyrokinesis," I whisper, failing to conceal the awe in my voice. Only the oldest and strongest Vampires are capable of such skills. Kilian responds only by closing his hand into a fist, extinguishing the flame. He no longer feels so hostile as he had seconds ago, so we stand in silence, facing the hearth. No way can this be called a comfortable silence, but it's not threatening either.

I gnaw on the edge of my lip, questions piling on one another. When did Annette die? How long had Kilian been sick before he'd given in to Tyran's seduction of life beyond the illness? Had it been cancer that had left him cadaverous and frail? Was that what Annette and his mother had died from?

Why had Kilian felt so threatened by the Gargoyles?

While Vampires and Gargoyles are both creatures of the night, neither willingly venturing in the daylight, the difference lies in their opinions of the value of human life. Gargoyles are protectors that exist to safeguard humanity from the dangers of the supernatural, even though, technically, they're also supernatural. Vampires are predators by nature.

The oldest Gargoyles, created by Catholic supernatural monks to protect cathedrals, are the strongest and have the power to inhale souls, including those of other Supernaturals. Vampires, though, don't have souls, which is why Korday had called Kilian an abomination. Korday didn't strike me as an ancient Gargoyle, though. Then again, he was the first Gargoyle I'd ever conversed with. My curious questions fall short of having seen Kilian's true form, the dying man of my dreams.

"I… I dreamt of you," I admit quietly, glancing at his profile. Beside me, he feels taller, the top of my head only reaching his chin. His jaw is angular and clenches before he turns his head to watch me watching him. His dark eyes reflect the gold of the flames, and I frown at the blush that instantly burns my face.

"My kind is capable of manipulating dreams," he reminds me in a bored tone like I wouldn't know that. I've been studying the supernatural world since Mama died, and Nana had to explain why it wasn't wise to reanimate her, no matter how much it hurt. Nana uprooted us from our home in Georgia, where Mama was born, to the Bayou of Louisiana, where Nana was born.

I learned enough from touching the oldest records of Supernaturals to know that manipulating dreams is a gift only achieved by the Ancients, and Kilian is too young to be an Ancient. Tyran, however, is more than capable of dream manipulation.

"These were not necessarily dreams," I clarify softly. "They were your memories." His brow furrows deeply before he turns his eyes away and presses his lips into thin lines of disapproval. Anxiety crawls up my throat, unsure whether I want to reveal the vulnerability of what I saw and experienced of his human life. I conclude that it's safer that he doesn't know how much I really know about him.

Instead, I ask, "Why did you kill that man?"

"Which one?" he asks caustically, and I flick my eyes to him, disturbed by his callousness. His attention is fixed on the brightly lit hearth, the shadow-flames dancing along the lines of his face.

I swallow hard and say, "The man whose face you smashed in."

"You chose wrong."

"Me? You gave me no choice in the matter!" He cuts me with indignant gray eyes, and I'm taken aback when his fangs drop from his gums, and he leans toward me with menace. It takes all my grit to not visibly flinch, though my jaw is clenched so tight it hurts.

"You chose the Gargoyle, so I killed a human."

"I…" I stammer, but he doesn't let me accuse him of forcing me to choose the lesser of two violent evils. He reaches out and

94

wraps his fingers around my neck, yanking me flush to him, then lifts me to my toes until we're eye-to-eye again. My heart pounds with fear, and I tremble from where he dangles me.

"I have spared your life long enough," Kilian threatens, his voice low and growly.

"Now Hunter, that's no way to treat a guest."

Kilian and I both turn our heads to the unexpected visitor, who stands at the doorway. A tall, elegant woman watches with amusement, her big, pale blue eyes smiling wider than her mauve lips. She's wearing a black pair of leather skinny-pants and a sheer black long-sleeve shirt that reaches up to her neck. A row of ruffles along the front seam barely covers her black bra. Even more impressive is her milky, white skin and luscious red hair. She's gorgeous! Her Australian accent adds to her beauty.

"Since she's still fully alive and you haven't bled her dry, perhaps you'd prefer to introduce us?" Kilian releases me roughly and steps away while I clumsily regain my balance, rubbing my sore neck.

"I would prefer not to," he grumbles. The woman laughs, crossing the room with the kind of grace and familiarity of a supernatural.

She extends a delicate hand toward me and says in a friendly manner, "Kali," then grabs my gloved fingers in her hand before I can pull away. I frown when she releases it, and I awkwardly slip both hands behind my back, and nervously nip at a piece of skin from my lip.

"S… Sarah," I lie, and Kilian's eyes cut to mine, but I look away. The woman tilts her head with interest, her eyes roaming over me like she's assessing whether I'm worthy of her attention.

"Well, S-sarah," she mocks, looking me over. "You're definitely *not* Hunter's type, so you can't be a pet. You're wearing too many clothes for that and, really, there's just too much of you to see unclothed, anyway." My cheeks burn, but I don't bother to respond. I'm no stranger to body-shaming.

"Back off, Kali," Kilian mumbles as he heads back toward the bed. I don't look away from Kali, who watches Kilian. Her taunting smile widens at his annoyance. I have no idea why he's even annoyed when she's insulting *me*.

Kali turns her eyes to me again, and they're mean, like a predator playing with its prey. It's another expression I recognize from growing up fat and insecure, and it's not just Supernaturals. Though Mama and Nana homeschooled me, there were occasions when I had to go out, wearing gloves no matter how hot the weather, to avoid touching anyone. Some people were sympathetic, perhaps assuming I had some kind of skin disease like Tyran had assumed. But others, especially kids my age, were as nasty as Kali is about to be.

"I don't understand, Hunter." She grimaces, her ugliness pinning me to the ground. "There's *nothing* attractive about this one." I wince like she's slapped me. I hadn't expected her to be straightforward like that. She glances at my gloved hands and chortles. Meanly.

"The gloves. Are they to hide sausage fingers?" She reaches out to grab my hand, and my eyes widen in fear, not because my hands aren't gloved but because she may try to rip the gloves off my hands.

Just as I'm about to jump away, Kilian grabs Kali's wrist from behind her, pressing against her back, and leans into her neck, warning in a dangerously low voice, "Back. Off." Kali's eerily reflective eyes fill with fear, and she turns her head slightly over her shoulder. Kilian releases her with a narrowing of his eyes, and she turns on him so quickly it's obvious she's not human.

"Who is she?" Kali asks tremulously. She turns her pale eyes on me and steps away, closer to Kilian, as if I'm the one who threatened her. "Who is she, Hunter? If she's this important to you, it means she's dangerous to me."

"Just leave her alone," Kilian replies. Even though the danger has gone out of his voice, Kali isn't convinced.

"She doesn't smell human. She smells strongly like you, but I assumed it was because you'd slept with her."

"I did sleep with her," Kilian replies dryly.

"You know what I mean!" she practically shrieks. She drops her eyes, takes a frustrating breath, and faces him again. Kilian opens a closet door and pulls out a silver buttoned-down shirt that matches his eyes before a mesmer.

"Then tell me what she is," Kali insists, more calmly. "She isn't human."

Kilian ignores her, pulling off the black shirt he'd worn, baring his naked back to me. The muscles ripple beneath his movements, and I hate that I'm ogling him. While I'd seen him

97

naked, fresh out of the shower, I'd barely seen him before slamming my eyes shut. That's definitely not the same as appreciating his nakedness.

Aislynn wraps her body around my ankles, and I peer down at her as she slips past my legs and stands near Kilian. I'm not sure why she keeps choosing him over me, but maybe it's because they're both Risen. For the first time in her life, she's found a kindred soul.

I snap my eyes back at Kali when she inhales sharply and curses. Her wide eyes are fixed on Aislynn, who glares back coolly, a low hiss rising from her small chest. Kilian buttons up his shirt and squats briefly to run his hand over her arching back, then whispers something to her in Esperanto. Aislynn leans into his hand and purrs loudly. I stare in surprise that a Vampire and a cat can actually be friends, and glare in jealousy that it's *my* cat he's befriending!

I squeak when Kali aggressively approaches with a predatory gait I've only seen in wolves, though she's not a Werewolf. She doesn't have the glint or innate power to be as impulsive or stubborn as a Werewolf.

I take a self-preserving step back, and Kilian immediately flips around to face us. Our eyes meet. Mine wide with worry, his black orbs of suppressed anger, narrowed and threatening. But he isn't mad at me.

Kali rounds on him before he can advance and accuses, "You see! You're angry at *me*, not her! Who is she, Hunter? Why is she more important to you than me when we've known each other for over a century? And what's with the cat? Cats hate Vampires! You hate *all* kinds of animals!" She pauses, apparently in stunned silence, as if Kilian had answered her question.

Maybe he's telepathic, too!

"By the gods, Hunter, are you her Sire?"

Now *I'm* stunned into silence. Hunter's gray eyes reach mine, cold and unrelenting, then turns away without answering her accusation. I wouldn't have answered either since it's a good enough front for both of us that she thinks I'm his fledgling rather than his Animator mistress. I don't want Kali to know anything about me, much less about the power I hold over her long-time friend. The ruse will be exposed when I don't show any signs of Turning, though.

"Oh, no," Kali mutters in shocked disbelief, more to herself than to us. "Hunter, you've never Sired and you shouldn't. Ever."

"Why not?" Kilian responds without much caring.

"Aside from the fact that Siring is strictly forbidden by the Vampire Court Council *and* the SupaCourt?" Kali replies sardonically. Kilian turns to her, his head tilted in curiosity, and she adds worriedly, "And *that* right there is why you can't have a fledgling! You don't care about anything or anyone. You'll kill her. She'll die."

"Everything and everyone dies." His response bothers me, but not as much as Kali's next words.

"Hunter, we've talked about this before. There's a darkness inside you I've never felt from anyone else, and you know I'm all about feeling. You're dark, darker than the rest of us. You harbor a fury Tyran can barely control." She steeples her fingers, folds them into each other, then puts them over her mouth. It's a nervous gesture, and I'm afraid of what it means. Why is this woman who's known Kilian for so long afraid of him? What is this darkness that

99

scares her so much as a supernatural? And what does that mean for me as a human?

"Does Tyran know you're here?"

"I suppose he does," Kilian answers her. "This *is* where we come to get away." She silently watches him as he crosses the room with a grace so natural to Vampires. His steps are measured, purposeful. But his fists clench and unclench, his eyes fixed on me, a beautiful bright gray I've already seen. I take a frightened step back because I suddenly know why he doesn't always obey me and why he has the ability to mesmer me when I'm his Mistress.

I surprise Kilian when I'm the one who closes the space between us, gets on my tiptoes, and whispers frightfully, "Which Demon possesses you?"

Kilian stops in his tracks, his eyes narrowing into small slits of simmering anger, and I know instantly I'm right. Because his eyes aren't black with anger, or red with hunger. They're a dark, striated burgundy that look sickly, the pupil small and smeared, diseased. These are the eyes I'd first seen when he'd woken me with his hands wrapped around my throat, his fangs exposed with intent, his anger burning bright. I hadn't seen them like this since that first glimpse, so hadn't made the connection.

These are Demon eyes, and not just any Demon.

"Wrath," I surmise in a quivering whisper, stepping away, needing to stretch the distance between me and it, because this is no longer Kilian. I glance at Kali, more worried for her life than mine. Wrath is loyal only to Itself, and It will kill her no matter how Kilian feels about her.

100

"Leave," Kilian commands Kali, his voice no lower and no louder than usual. But darker. Scarier. "Now."

Kali is stunned for seconds before she runs out of the room, followed by a very frightened Aislynn. The door slams shut, and I'm frozen in place, too scared to run, knowing Kilian will see it as a hunt and Wrath will kill me as prey.

I wrack my brain, trying to recall any incantation to ward off Demons, but the words and manuscripts jumble in my frightened brain, scrambling the messages. My chest and throat grow tight, and I force myself to breathe, if only to recite the only power I hold over Kilian.

"Rule number one," I say, my voice shaky with each dangerous step he takes toward me. "You cannot hurt me. I, your Mistress, command it."

"No," he growls, as he'd done countless times before.

"Rule number two," I continue, swallowing hard. "You must obey every one of my directives. Every single one."

"No," he growls again, but the sound is different, lower, darker. Because it's not one voice that refuses my command. It's the sound of multiple voices speaking at once, the souls of the damned along the riverbanks of hell.

"Rule number three," I squeak fearfully, but directly to Wrath, who closes the space between us with unnatural speed. "If my life ends, Kilian's life ends, too, and you'll lose the body you've possessed." Kilian stops abruptly, scowling deeply, like the wrinkled face of a rabid beast ready to rip into flesh. I blink back tears as Wrath stares at me while Kilian's face distorts, blurring for momentarily where Wrath's form is a hazy mist behind Kilian's frame.

Its fire-red color is the most distinct aspect of the Demon. It practically glows with hell-darkness in contrast to Kilian's pale skin. But the rest of It is even more horrific. Long, jutting horns like those of a goat above large, pointed ears, an atrocity between an Elf and a bat. A snout with four sharp fangs, thicker than a Vampire's, two on top and two on the bottom of Its gaping mouth. A naked body of corded muscle with Cervidae feet. Bony wings, lacking any membrane but fluttering behind It, clawed at each bony end.

It's terrifying, and I shudder.

"You are *not* my Mistress," the Demon announces. The voices send shivers up my spine as if Wraith were ripping it out, vertebrae by vertebrae. I force my mind to recall all the historical references to Wrath, from the revelation of the seven deadly sins to the fourth century monk Evagrius Ponticus, to the documentation of their purgatory and prison by Dante Alleghieri. The photographic memory I inherited from Mama is about to save my life!

"You've possessed Kilian's body for centuries, sparing you the hassle of finding another willing host," I coax, though I can't imagine why or when Kilian had given the Demon such allowances. "Pride, after all, is not your sin but your *brother's.*"

Wrath hisses, misty spittle flying out of Its mouth, landing nowhere since Wrath is only an illusion without corporeal form meant to frighten. That's why It requires a body. Otherwise, It's condemned to reign in a kingdom of Its own making, overlooking the drowning souls that furiously fight one another for Its attention, while It watches with aberrant contempt.

Even though It's just a red-hazed mirage, Wrath scares the hell out of me!

"But I am *his* Mistress, and you need him alive," I inform It, my voice shaky and I swallow hard, unsure what It'll do to me.

We stare at each other, Wrath's rage simmering in Kilian's streaked, burgundy eyes. Slowly, the sickly striation fades to black orbs until Kilian is staring back at me with silvery eyes. I exhale the breath I'm holding and nearly burst into tears.

"You forgot the rule about dying when you do," Kilian spats bitterly. He speaks in his normal voice, deep and grumbly, not in Wrath's creepy ones. I regard my Risen carefully, because he seems unaware of the Demon that possesses him. I *had* mentioned the final rule, distinctly directed at Wrath. My heart clenches in pity for the Vampire who isn't just some Risen. He's *my* Risen and, for the first time since I gave him my essence, I care about Kilian's wellbeing.

I didn't hear the last thing Kilian said, but am sure it's probably another defiant threat, so I simply respond, "You need constant reminders, since you're a rebellious Risen." The response is *definitely* not the one he expects because he frowns impressively. I force myself to ignore its dangerous meaning. Knowing that he's the lesser of two evils, I amble to the door and add, "I'm hungry. I hope Kali is preparing breakfast." Kilian grunts and mumbles in Esperanto while following me out.

It turns out Kali *can't* cook for humans. She explains that, as a Succubus, she feeds on sexual energy, not breakfast meals. As a Seer, I have no interest in sex since it means exposing myself and absorbing other people's experiences and memories. I'm not interested in adding Kali's scandalous Succubus experiences to my eclectic repertoire compared to my prude ones. Kilian's memories and experiences are nightmare enough!

However, Kilian is an excellent cook, which fascinates me since he doesn't need physical nourishment because he feeds on blood. Apparently, he enjoys the activity of eating.

"My senses are heightened," he'd grumbled when I watched him eat with amusement. "Human food satisfies the gustatory sense. The taste of blood is different for each race, and I'm selective with human blood, since its sweetness varies."

His wolfish smile knocks mine down when he'd adds, "Yours is the sweetest blood I've ever tasted." I frown, but then Aislynn jumps up onto my lap, leans into my warmth, and falls asleep on my lap. Kilian and I sit in silence while we eat, watching Aislynn's body rise and fall with her breathing.

When the sun hides beneath the horizon and the shadows stretch from the thick curtains along every window of the two-story cabin, Kilian and Kali speak in hushed voices, considerably heightening my anxiety. Kali is still upset by my presence and Kilian's loyalties and wants to wait for Tyran to arrive. Kilian wants to leave, though he hasn't told her why he needs to leave or where he's going.

I want to leave as well and get to Nana as soon as possible, though my primary objective for reaching Nana has changed. I want to free Kilian from Wrath first, *then* break his Risen bond to me. He deserves to be free. From both of us.

I slip out of the kitchen while they speak and head towards the front door, hoping to make a hasty escape. Aislynn sits by my feet, staring into the hallway that leads back to the kitchen, waiting for her new best friend. We're both startled when the front door flies open and Tyran steps in like it's his home, which it must be since Vampires have to be invited into a home before waltzing in. Aislynn runs off with a screech, bounding up the stairs and disappearing into the hall. I'm annoyed that the door wasn't even locked!

Tyran's eyes meet mine and panic hits me that the Vampire Sire has found us. His intentions for being here are unclear because my presence pits his caring for Kilian against his own ambitions. I'm a threat to what he holds dear and what needs to be done.

I turn to run and slam into Kilian's chest. He grabs my shoulders and carefully steadies me while my heart chases after each breath. When he gently sets me beside him, his protectiveness helps take the edge off my fear—a little. I peer at his chiseled face in surprise and gratitude, but his serious gaze is on Tyran. Worry that I'm pitting him against his Sire worms into my consciousness even though his eyes are gray and cool, not angry or black. Or Demon-infected.

I turn to find Tyran regarding me and not him.

"Hello, Suri," he says in a friendly manner. "I hope Kilian and Kali have been treating you well."

I temper my fear, refusing to show him what I'm sure he can smell, and reply, "As well as they can."

He chuckles congenially, confusing me because I still can't figure out his intentions. He has so much more to gain by delivering me to the Vampire Courts Council or the SupaCourt than helping me. Then again, if he delivers me before releasing Kilian, Kilian is likely to kill while protecting me and get killed in the process.

Tyran proves that he cares about him too much to rush my delivery when he finally lifts his gaze to Kilian, warmth filling the blue pools of his eyes.

"I hope you didn't scare Suri too much, Hunter."

"I scared Kali more than the Necromancer," he replies, his tone light.

I sidestep the two men when Tyran says with sincere concern, "Why? What happened?" He doesn't wait for an answer and quickly searches for Kali, disappearing into the cabin to find her. I watch his departure, lingering on the unexpected response.

While I have a lot of information about the supernatural world, I know little about their interactions with one another. I simply assumed they maintained friendships and intimacies with their own race. Friendships are more like mutually beneficial business arrangements than emotional attachments.

Then again, perhaps Tyran's relationship with the Succubus is just mutual sexual pleasure. What would I know?

"When are we leaving?" I ask Kilian hesitantly. He drops his eyes to mine, cool, dispassionate glimmers of control, then pensively peers over my head. Silent for a few moments, I wait for his fractured mind to respond rather than react. I'm not sure how influential Wrath is on his decision-making, or if it's just a reaction to his anger. Either way, I'll patiently wait for Kilian to adjust to his new supernatural status as a Risen while unknowingly being possessed by a Demon.

Tyran returns, followed by Kali, who's still beautiful despite another impressive frown. She regards me with uncertainty, and I

106

hope Tyran wasn't careless enough to reveal why I'm important to Kilian. Or who I am at all.

Tyran declares, "It's time for you to leave. I came to make sure you were both safe and evidently, you are."

"I can take care of myself," Kilian says with slight annoyance. Tyran's brotherly smile irks Kilian until Tyran's green eyes fall on me, then I turn back to him.

"And her as well," Kilian adds with growing annoyance, crossing his arms.

Tyran chuckles and teases, "I know, Hunter. You have no other choice, even against those closest to you."

"I knew it," Kali mumbles with accusation. "He *did* Sire her." She shakes her head and stomps away with disapproval. As I follow her with my eyes, I'm not sure why Kilian Siring me would bother her so much, or why it annoys me as much as it does. What *is* her relationship with him? Are they all friends? More concerning, however, is why I care about what her relationship with him is. Kilian is my Risen, not my boyfriend!

Tyran follows Kali with his eyes, the amusement gone from his expression, and it's strange to see warmth and affection in his eyes.

I jump into Kilian's awkward arms when the house plunges us into darkness. More appropriately, plunges *me* into darkness since they can see in the dark. This time, Kilian wraps his arms around my shoulders, pulling me closer. The move is both comforting and strange, and I glance up but can't see him and don't know why we're suddenly standing in darkness. I jump when his lips whisper cool words against my ear.

"The supernatural world is one of Balance, which is why every race has its Court Council and Supernaturals are monitored by the SupaCourt. They maintain the balance of power or, more accurately, a semblance of it since all governments are subjected to corruption.

"Supernatural gifts are also one of balance. The life you give, Necromancer, is also the life you take. You forced life into me, and now must pay the consequences of taking one. I suggest you use your gift to keep us alive."

I tremble when he growls the last words.

Every supernatural record, often presumed as myth or moral storytelling by humans, indicates the balance that keeps life and death evenly distributed in the mortal world. While Blinking leaves a trace, Animating gives life to the dying and takes it from the living. Oftentimes, it's a random person, but sometimes, as in the case of Mama, it's someone I love. She'd taken her life at the end because I'd given it to Aislynn. The balance of Psychometry, though, is as frightening as that of Necromancy.

Precognition.

Kilian's presence moves away, and I inhale nervously, his scent surrounding me, stirring a memory, but not enough to bring up the images. I breathe him in again, trying to recapture that memory. Wood ash. There's something sweet beneath the sylvan that teases my senses. Maple syrup, maybe?

When I inhale again, trying to identify the scent beneath the maple syrup and wood ash, Kilian's voice rumbles, "Stop that." He's so close a puff of his breath smoothens the creases of my forehead because his voice is low and gravelly, but not dark and violent.

A feeling stirs in my chest, then slips down my belly in sweet, unexpected ripples. I'm suddenly very aware of his arms still holding me, his muscled body, and impressive height. I'm not sure if I'm more afraid of his reminder of the inevitable balance of my gifts, the flurry of movement that surrounds me in the darkness, or the fleeting tug of attraction that hits me with as much surprise as the darkness does.

"Did anyone follow you from the Celosia Court?" Tyran asks, his voice calling from a distance, like he's in another room. His voice pokes at my attraction with mockery, pulling me away from Kilian, though not physically. Kilian is still the lesser of all evils.

"We met up with a Gargoyle," Kilian replies. Tyran growls, and the sound is so feral and so much closer I freeze, the primitive side of my brain kicking into action again.

"Which one?" The animosity in each word snaps like a rubber band; the venom of hate is distinct.

"Korday."

I inhale sharply, frowning in surprise. How does Killian know Korday? Is that why he was so angry that I'd chosen the safety of the Gargoyle over him?

As if reading my mind, Kilian confirms, "You chose wrong, Necromancer." While Tyran is running around the house in quick swooshes of air and minimal noise, Kilian still holds me.

"My name is Suri, Kilian," I retort quietly, and he grunts an order to not call him that. We both know my bravado is only a front to hide my growing apprehension that the Gargoyles may have found us. Whether that's a good thing or a bad thing is still unclear, but I don't want it to be at the expense of Kilian's life.

"He's too far from his resting place to be here," Tyran counters, his voice so close I tremble against Kilian. The friendly and cordial Tyran is replaced by the Vampire Ancient, that he truly is. Not the cunning one whose suave demeanor could win over any Court, but one of the oldest living Vampire Ancients in modern history.

That's it! That's his intention! He'd rather help us escape from other Courts, including the SupaCourt, because he has more power than any one being should have, *especially* if he controls a Ternion who can give him the power of life and knowledge.

"The closest Gargoyle clan is at the Kygore Cathedral twenty miles away."

Tyran snorts, moving away, and says with disdain, "As if the deities need any more protection."

"They don't protect the gods. They protect humans *for* the gods."

"As if the gods care about humans. They're simply the guiding force of our destiny, putting us on a path that's already been predestined."

"Well, yes," Kali replies impatiently. Ugh! Why the hell was she back? "But it's the choices they make that drive them along that path, Tyran. The end may be predetermined, but how you get there is solely up to you."

"Easy for you to say, youngling," Tyran shares, his voice soft and intimate. The contemplative silence that follows allows me some seconds to think on Kali's words because I never thought about my destiny. I always assumed my gifts were flukes of nature or a matter of genetics and inheritance. It had only resulted in a life of isolation and loneliness. That life ended when I extended Kilian's, and I can't help but wonder whether the path that destined us to meet was his, or mine.

Kilian releases me from his embrace, grabs my hand in his, and pulls me away from the front door, saying, "Stop biting your lip. It'll bleed an invitation." I quickly release my lip, reluctantly disappointed when I hear him exhale a laugh I didn't get to see. "Time to go."

"Where are we going?"

"Humans and their questions," Kilian grumbles.

"We're bringing Aislynn, right?" He grunts and imitates my soft whistle for her. It annoys me, especially when I feel Aislynn brush my leg and purr.

"If Kilian dies, will you die with him?" Tyran asks from behind us. I trip over my own feet, but Kilian holds me up. I have no idea how to answer Tyran's question because I don't know whether Kilian's death would be mine as well. I'd never thought about the Risen's life expectancy since I never intended to have one, other than Aislynn.

"I don't know," I say honestly. "But I don't want to take a chance."

"And why wouldn't you want to take a chance with Kilian's life, Suri?" Tyran challenges, not unkindly. "Don't you want to break your bond with him?"

"Not at the expense of his life," I declare with affront. "If I wanted him dead, I would've never animated him!" Silence splits the moment like an arrow. Kilian's hand stiffens around mine and Tyran's movements stop completely while I'm left breathless in the limbo. Something shifts in whatever dynamic exists between the three of us and begins a ripple effect I'm afraid might stretch too far.

"She's a Necro!" Kali nearly shrieks, shattering the glassy moment, and I exhale sharply, uncertain about what just happened but knowing that we felt it.

"I prefer Animator," I mumble out of rote.

"Dammit, Hunter. You didn't kill this one?!" The comment slams against my chest, wrecking the connection I'd felt only seconds earlier. I'm painfully aware that the darkness that surrounds me goes beyond just being able to see because it has little to do with seeing in the dark like it does about living in it.

I pull my hand from Kilian's and mutter in trembling, "What do you mean by 'this one'?"

If Kilian hunts Necromancers, it means he's a Black Heart assassin, and, if he's a Black Heart assassin, then I should've never lived! Dammit, I should've unpacked all his damn memories, so I'd know that!

I'd read about the Black Heart assassins in the Vampyre manuscripts, though most of them are written in Esperanto, a language I can't seem to figure out no matter how adept I've become as a linguist of ancient, supernatural languages. Enochian is *definitely* much easier to learn!

The Black Hearts had been an elite group of supernatural hunters who assassinated hard-to-kill targets. They'd been disbanded centuries ago when the stronger supernatural races formed an alliance. Rather than hunting each other for power, each race formed thirteen Courts in every major city led by the most powerful in their race. A supernatural representative from each race is chosen to be a councilman for the SupaCourt on behalf of their race.

It was intended to be a sharing of power, not devoid of political overtures that plague every form of government, but one that keeps their world hidden from the humans to maintain the balance. Plenty in the records indicate that the Black Hearts had begun hunting Necromancers before the SupaCourt was established. The reasoning, though, varies per race.

But why would they continue to hunt Necromancers when the Black Hearts had been disbanded? Then again, I can see Kilian continuing the practice. No. Not Kilian. I can see Wrath killing us off, one by one, in a violent attempt to maintain the balance without affecting the Demon's current existence. If a Necromancer gives life, but doesn't take it, then the Demon, in its uncontrollable anger and drive to not return to the fifth circle of hell, takes the life of the one who gives it.

Right now, I'm its only unbalance.

Except, in having taken its host's life, the Demon's desperation for balance backfired, leaving me alive and in control.

No wonder Kilian has bitten me so often, even though he can't feed from me because of the Risen Code. Wrath is the one causing the rebellion!

Enrapt in my thoughts, I scream when someone grabs my elbow to push me forward. Shuffling away, I bang my shin against an unseen piece of furniture, biting back a curse. My eyes roam wildly in my head, searching for any light that could help guide me out of the house. But only darkness meets my terrified gaze.

"There's nowhere to run when you can't see," Kilian whispers in my ear, cynical and dark. I scramble clumsily away, only to run into a giggling Kali who pushes me roughly, most likely finding sport in tormenting me.

But my panic goes into override when I envision her reaching out to remove my gloves, exposing me to her entire existence. I'll be stuck reliving her sordid experiences, intermingled with Kilian's violent ones: sex, blood, and violence. Just the thought has me running to keep my distance from her and Tyran, wherever he is, whose past existence is more dangerous than the other two combined!

I turn to my left and end up slamming my forehead against a doorframe with enough force it momentarily stuns me. My head bursts with lights like confetti, and I groan from the sharp pain, warm blood trickling down the side from where the corner of the frame met my forehead.

Kilian snarls viciously and wraps his arms around my shoulders, pressing my back flush against his chest with the possessiveness I've only seen in Aislynn. He growls in Esperanto, his voice dark and menacing, rumbling through me. Tyran replies in the same language, his voice calm but cutting, sharper than Kilian's.

My Risen exhales with frustration and drops his arms.

I squeal when he flips me around so fast my stomach lurches, and my head spins. Red lights suddenly strobe through the house, and panic slams into my chest, ripping out chunks of my fast-pounding heart. Though I can only see in quick flashes, at least I can see where everyone is, though I wish I couldn't.

In several blinks, I make out Tyran standing several feet away, near the stairwell to the second floor. In his left hand, he holds the hilt of a long, wide sword, which is the most out-of-place item in the cabin, aside from me. His green eyes glare black as death in the red light, eerily fixed on me.

In another blink, Kali moves closer to us from the back of the cabin. Each flash of the red lights closes the distance between us. While Tyran's attention is on me, hers is on him, her expression tight with worry. She flicks her attention briefly to Kilian, then me and back to him, and mouths one word that sends a cold shaft of fear straight through me.

Blood.

I turn to Kilian, his silvery eyes dropping from Kali to me, dominating my attention. His jaw is set, and his lips hard-pressed. I'm not sure if it's anger or fear that I see on his face. Or maybe, inexplicably, a little of both?

He grabs my face between cold hands and pulls my head toward him like he's going to kiss me. My heart pounds with the same rhythm as the cut on my head, and I'm not sure if I'd let him kiss me or punch him in the throat!

"Don't move," he warns, leaning toward me. Breathing stills in my chest, snared back by stark fear. I'm afraid Wrath is about to take advantage of this moment to break through the Risen Order and kill the Necromancer who's unbalanced Its existence. "And don't scream. Or I'll make you run like the fleeing prey all humans are."

I close my eyes, a wave of nauseating fear crushing me. Tears gather along the edges of my eyes, and I inhale sharply when the coolness of his tongue brushes along my temple where a door frame had ended my pathetic attempt at escape. Kilian groans deep in his throat as he laps up the blood, his fingers painfully digging into my face. My stomach clenches tightly as tears slip down my cheek. When the pointed edge of his fangs graze against the skin on my forehead, I croak his name in a trembling whisper in hopes my Risen will hear the voice of his Mistress and adhere to the code.

"Kilian."

Chapter 9: Gargoyles (Kilian)

"Kilian."

Through the blood haze of the sweetest, most intoxicating blood I'd ever tasted, I hear the Necromancer's voice speak my name. My real name. The one I'd discarded when I died the first time. The name only she calls me when she'd given me a third chance at life. The one that subdues my innate nature to feed from her!

I pull my tongue away from her forehead and slowly lick my lips, savoring the last drops of blood. It only makes me yearn for more of it, though. I reluctantly slide my tongue over the tip of my fangs, willing it to retract, against all reason save obedience to a Mistress I don't want to obey!

The light alarms revealed Tyran hungrily staring at the Necromancer's cut. He'd deeply inhaled the scent of her blood and closed his green eyes in anxious pleasure to open black ones that glared with blood lust. While I was bound to the Risen Code not to feed from her, Tyran wasn't.

My protectiveness to the Mistress threatened to choke me!

I had to remind Tyran that the Code bound me to protect, and he replied that his Vampire nature may be one we shared but that I was too young to understand its depth. As much as I hated to admit it, his response burned. I had not chosen to be the Risen of the clumsiest, most insufferable, and intoxicating Necromancer I've ever targeted!

I had to clear the air of her blood scent before Tyran reached her. I needed to avoid attacking him, which would leave him with no choice but to kill me because I'm no match against a Vampire Ancient like Tyran. Then again, I hoped I was more faithful to him as my Sire and friend than to her as my Mistress and enemy!

Despite having her fear knock against my ribcage with a force that compelled me to hold her in my arms and escape the safehouse, I licked the blood from her forehead, barely able to protect her from me. Only the sound of my name on her lips had kept me from feeding. I step away from the Necromancer in search of Tyran, purposely ignoring the way her soft sobs bother me, twist inside me like a coiled serpent waiting to strike. Kali must've taken Tyran while I teased my palate with the Necromancer's blood because they're nowhere in sight.

"We leave now," I inform her and reach for her hand, but she yanks it away. I glare with impatience. "I have no time for your foolishness."

"How many Necromancers have you killed?" she asks, her voice stronger than I expect after her sobbing. She lifts her eyes to mine, not mud brown as I prefer to see them because it highlights her humanity and defeat. These eyes are a bright amber that demands a reply.

I frown and force out, "I have no time—"

"How many?" she insists angrily, taking me aback. I stare at her, strangely excited by her anger instead of annoyed. I frown, unaccustomed to the response.

"Too many to count," I purposely reply with vague disregard.

"How many?" she orders, the two words given in two separate forceful breaths. I grin wolfishly, her anger and demand drawing my fangs. Not to feed. Not to intimidate. But to impress.

"One hundred forty-one," I reveal with pride. "None made it past the age of thirty-two." Her eyes widen, her ruddy cheeks paling, and my grin turns smug, because she's thirty-two. My smile stiffens with unease when her eyes narrow and anger kindles brightly.

"You hinted that I'd chosen Korday over you back at the diner," she says. I bite back the snarl at the mention of the Gargoyle's name, the same Gargoyle who's tried to save Necromancers from me in the past. And had always failed.

"You told me I'd made the wrong choice and that my decision had been the reason for the death of the man with the glasses." I stare with boredom because I have no idea which man she's referring to, and don't care.

The Necromancer straightens her back, sniffs the last of her pathetic sobs, and lifts her chin. I would've gloated in her anger if her eyes weren't drawing me in, captivating me, mesmerizing me, stealing my will and identity, and twisting it into something hers. I'm trapped in the power of her command, struggling to fight against her next words.

"This time, *I* make my own choice. I will step out the front door, and you will not follow." I growl a rejection, but she continues undaunted. "I will Blink away and seek refuge among my own. Not with you. Not with Korday. Not with any Court or any supernatural. You *will not* find me."

119

"You are bonded to me by blood," I remind her with cold anger. "I will always find you."

"You will try because it's in your nature," she replies, her eyes softening while mine hardens. But she's edging closer to the door, making me increasingly tense. I'm faster than her, but not if she Blinks before I reach her.

"Your Blink will leave a trace," I remind her. "Every Supernatural will follow the trail wherever you go." She frowns, not having considered the long-term effects of a quick escape. I narrow my eyes, drop my tone, and warn, "And I will always be the one to find you."

She slips her lower lip between her teeth and bites, unwittingly sucking on it, and that's all I can take! I rush to her with inhuman speed, roughly grab her by the neck, and yank her to me, her toes barely touching the floor. Her eyes, the size of saucers, widen more in surprise than fear.

"If you Blink," I warn threateningly, "I'm coming with you, even if it means grabbing you by the neck for the rest of your mortal life." I scowl, more as a show of power than of anger. She may be my Mistress, but I'm still in control!

"You're not going anywhere until you release me!" I remind her pointedly. She turns her eyes away, almost contritely, like she'd forgotten that the only reason she's still alive is because I'm bound to her and because I'll die if she dies.

"Let's go," I order and, still holding her by the neck, throw open the door in time to hear Tyran yell out, "*I, too, am not a bit tamed!*" A dangerous smile slits my face when he throws one of the Quernbiter swords over to me.

Grabbing it in one hand and dragging the Necromancer with the other, I reply loudly, "*I, too, am untranslatable!*"

"Really?" the Necromancer says with annoyance. "You're quoting Walt Whitman?"

I can't help admiring her vast knowledge of just about everything, including the quote Tyran and I always cite when we fight together, in memory of Tyran's long-time poet and friend. But I don't have time to unpack the thought of admiring the Necromancer because there are Gargoyles outside the cabin, waiting to draw us out.

A Gargoyle in its full supernatural form is a formidable opponent. They're double the size of a human body builder with a wingspan double the size of Tyran's. They have three-toed feet with sharp claws on each and matching claws on their five-fingered hands. The features that frighten humans the most are the nubby horns on their heads and their rat-like tails, as thick as human arms. Their gray skin is darker than the stone from which they're made and imprisoned in during the day. While Vampires sleep in their true form, the form in which they died, Gargoyles are fully aware inside a stone prison. Watching. Listening. Frozen until sundown.

A Gargoyle races toward us, a double-bladed, folding ax clutched in his massive hand, the kind I haven't seen in at least two centuries. The sound of metal against metal clangs around us, echoing in the courtyard in front of the cabin.

With the Necromancer firmly held in one hand and the sword in the other, I wait for the Gargoyle to reach me before I lift the sword, purl it twice, and meet my opponent's blow. It's a powerful strike and the muscles on my arm tense from the impact. It's been a long while since I've used a sword, considering firearms and knives are the weapon of choice nowadays.

Gargoyles aren't affected by contemporary weapons of choice, though. Guns and knives don't penetrate their bodies because the stone absorbs and redistributes the force. Quernbiter swords, however, were forged in the Norwegian quarries where they could cut a millstone in half. It can also cut a Gargoyle in half.

The Necromancer screams when I move us away from the next attack, my wrist snapping powerfully as I twist the sword and slice through the Gargoyle's arm. The stone limb and ax fall to the ground with a crack and crumble at the Gargoyle's feet. A cement-like substance oozes out of the Gargoyle's missing limb, and the Necromancer screams again. I squeeze her neck and strangle the scream.

"Stop yelling," I warn dangerously, and she nods quickly, blinking away tears. Her terror strikes me like lighting, slithering under my skin like hooked bore worms. I loosen my grip in discomfort, remembering the time I'd been buried alive with the bore worms for nearly thirty years before Tyran found me.

For a short moment, I turn to watch Tyran being attacked by four of the largest Gargoyles in the clan. His green eyes are bright with amusement, and his lip slightly tilt in a smirk that only angers the Gargoyles, which he's very aware of. He displays the speed and skill only an Ancient could ever have, a blur that slices and maims but doesn't kill. Killing is too quick. Maiming can be watched, an art appreciated. The Gargoyles, with their self-righteousness and conscience, are no match for him.

Impressed and slightly distracted, the Necromancer squeaks in a strangled voice, "Watch out!" I nearly roll my eyes, offended that she presumes I can't hear the two Gargoyles behind me! I move the hand from her neck to her waist, pull her flush against me, and twirl us around, Quernbiter slicing through the gut of the first Gargoyle, cement oozing from his innards. Cut in half, both parts instantly turn to stone and crumble into pieces.

The other Gargoyle reaches out for the Necromancer and my amusement turns protectively ugly. I cut her extended arm right off before she touches her, then twist around, the Necromancer's breath catching, and sever the Gargoyle's head in one swoop. She drops unceremoniously, the entire body turning to stone and disintegrating around us.

"Hunter!" Kali's voice screams from beyond the court. There's an urgency in her voice, one I hadn't heard from her in all the decades we've known each other. My eyes catch hers, panicked, just as she raises them above my head. I glance up in time to see a large net, held by four Gargoyles, drop over me.

My first mistake was not speeding out of the way. But I'm holding a mortal in my arms, one I couldn't kill even if I wanted to, and the speed would've crushed her organs. Instead, I let the net fall over us as I pull her against me, wrapping my arms around her and blocking her from the bulk of the net.

My second mistake was having exposed myself for the sake of sparing a human. The net is made of silver and the moment it touches my body, it instantly burns through the clothing down to my skin. I howl in pain and fall to my knees as the net closes in around me. The silver burns through my hair and face, the smell of sulfur and charcoal filling the space between me and the Necromancer. The

123

net is designed to shrink and tighten to capture Supernaturals allergic to silver.

Like Vampires.

"No, no, no," the Necromancer mutters repeatedly, then surprises me when she squeezes her large body from under me and pushes the offensive silver off my skin. "Stop! Please! Don't hurt him!" As the net tightens, the Necromancer's body presses against mine. She pushes the net away from my skin, climbs on my back to cover as much of me as possible, and continues to scream for the Gargoyles to stop.

"Call off the other Vampires," a familiar voice orders. "And we'll spare his life."

Korday.

"*Futue te ipsum!*" I curse him in Latin, the language of Gargoyles. I can't see Korday, the pressure of the Necromancer tightening over me. Her body lays heavy and protective over mine, but the silver net wraps around us and beneath me, touching my exposed hands. I growl in anger and indignation.

"Don't go near them, Tyran, or I'll blow the net," Korday warns darkly. I can't see my friend, but I can feel the heat of his anger.

"You?" he mocks in a deceptively calm voice. "Kill a human? I highly doubt it."

"I will kill a Vampire," Korday reasons. "And *you* will be the reason the human dies."

Tyran laughs, completely devoid of humor, and scoffs, "I could care less about the death of another human."

"You do with this one," Korday declares. "She's the only Ternion in this hemisphere. Only one of three in every generation." The Necromancer's body stiffens, and the air around us is so tense it's electric. The hostility is as palpable as the revelation.

"Do you swear an oath on the Church that you will spare his life and theirs?" the Necromancer bargains in a loud, confident voice, startling me. The short silence confirms it shocks them, too.

"Call them off before we're forced to kill them all," Korday restates in a hard voice. I feel the Necromancer shiver at his tone, and the urge to kill him burns hotter than the net.

"*Dimitte me!*" I growl to be released. The vibration in my chest echoes much deeper, where something else is a greater threat than I am. If it's released, though, the Necromancer is as dead as the rest of them, and I can't allow it.

"Do you swear an oath on the Church that created you to protect humanity that you and your clan will spare his life and the lives of the others?" she cries out, then moans as the net tightens. She wraps her arms around my neck and presses her forehead against my temple. The gesture feels intimate. Personal. Precious.

"Kilian," she whispers, her breath fanning my face. I shiver at the sound of my name in her hushed voice, the feel of her body against mine, the concern that shakes and shifts my foundation.

"Don't speak," she pleads. "Loosen your body because the tension hurts all over." A tightening in my chest forces me to loosen my muscles and give her some room to breathe. She exhales heavily, and relief floods me that I've alleviated some of her pain. Not because I care about her, but because she cares about me.

"I won't let them kill you," she continues. "But I need you to trust me. Don't lose yourself in its anger." Her last words are clearer than her well-intentioned assurances. Control and protectiveness war within me against the warmth of her body, the exhale of her breath on my skin, the conviction in her voice that she'll save me. Again.

The flapping of too many wings echoes in the night sky. Surrounding us. Threatening us. A snarl rumbles from inside me, too deep inside, and I force it down, especially when Suri groans loudly, the sound grating and tense.

"Korday!" she cries out, her voice revealing her suffering. "You were created and called by the Church to protect me, but the net you cast hurts! Swear an oath on your creators that you and your clan won't kill him or the others! Swear it!"

The flapping intensifies, running footsteps coming closer, my fury turning ugly. Long, sharp claws stretch and shove through my fingers. I scrape them against the net that leashes me. But not even my claws are immune to the pain and strength of silver, smoking along with the rest of my exposed skin. It won't kill me, though, and that will be the Gargoyles' mistake when I return and kill Korday and his entire clan!

A loud yowl startles everyone, especially when a Gargoyle cries out at the same time the Necromancer screams, "Don't kill her! No!"

Aislynn! While I hate cats, I liked her. She willingly liked me, too, and though neither of us understood the connection, we appreciated each other. Her yowl is followed by growls and screeching until it's suddenly silenced.

"No!"

I'm not sure which of us cried the word louder, but the Necromancer and I both feel the death of the Risen cat at the same time. Suri sobs against my neck, her tears collecting between my shoulder blades and conscience. I vow to kill Korday, even if it isn't today, then force myself to relax as supernaturally as possible so I don't add to Suri's pain.

"Agreed," Korday finally says, and I swallow down the anger. "But you both come with us, and the others must not engage us anymore."

"No!" I refuse fiercely when Suri's sobs turn louder, a ceremonial drum beating in my head.

"Then you will die with the others, except for the human," Korday threatens. My fangs grow and scrape against my gums from both sides of my mouth, pushing them further than when I feed. Long, thick tusks ready to tear his flesh apart.

"We agree to your terms," Suri replies in a broken-down voice that cuts me like the net. "Please, just release us."

"Not with a conscious Vampire," Korday replies, his voice as obstinate as his resolve. The sound of multiple feet encircles us, and I thrash angrily, barely able to contain my Demon. I force it down again when Suri cries out, her tears hotter than my burning skin.

Tyran's speed is unmatched, catching the Gargoyles by surprise as screams erupt around us at his merciless attack. But Suri and I both know there are too many Gargoyles attacking at once.

"No, Tyran!" Suri screams, her voice piercing through the violence in distress. "Please let us go. Please. He's still alive! They'll kill him, too!" She hiccups another sob but continues. "Korday swore an oath that he and his clan won't hurt him, or you and Kali. But you have to let us go with them, so you can find us later."

I can't see Tyran's expression, can't see where he's standing, or if he's even listening. But I definitely feel the heat of his anger rippling in waves that make Suri whimper against me. Panic and fear stumble out of me, and I call out to Tyran in Esperanto.

"We will go with the Gargoyles, then kill them together when I break out."

"Can your Mistress be trusted?" he replies, his voice low and vicious. His fury is hot and alive, but he's still in control. When my fury burns, there's no control. There's only violence and death. Suri is different.

Though I'm bound to her as Risen, it doesn't mean trust is automatic. But she demanded an oath from the Gargoyles to save our lives, even after the death of one Risen. Or perhaps because she didn't want to lose the life of her other Risen. While my intention had always been forcing her to release me from the Risen bond, then finish my mission, she has changed my objective.

"Yes," I reply. The whooshing sound of his speed startles the Gargoyles into an anxious frenzy.

Tyran crouches beside me and confides to Suri in a barely contained voice, "I entrust my most loyal friend, blood brother, and only family to you. If you betray him, I'll make you the most miserable pawn in my rise to power. I will deprive you of the release of death, and you will wish for it every day of your miserable mortal life."

His heartfelt words startle me because we've never spoken of the love we have for each other. He's never been my Sire because he's always been my friend and brother. Suri's words, though, are just as startling.

"As you are Dubhshláin O'Catháin, dark challenger of the Celtic wilds, I swear to protect him as diligently as he has no choice in protecting me," she vows. I can't see Tyran's expression, but I'm sure he's as shocked as I am that she knows his real name, the one he was born with, the one he abandoned like I abandoned mine.

"If not me," she continues. "Then Wrath will assure it. We have a mutual agreement that will keep him alive." The revelation hangs between the three of us as it did when she'd admitted she'd never put me in danger for the sake of her own life.

"I hope it doesn't come to that," Tyran responds. "Wrath will kill you both."

She puffs out a shaky breath and adds, "I may prefer that over your threat. At least the Demon's uncontrollable rage will be quick whereas yours will feel like eternity." Tyran doesn't reply. He reaches between the small holes in the net, his hand immediately smoking from the silver, and pats my hand.

"Stay alive, brother, for life would be eternally boring without you." I smile, my fangs receding at his warmth. He moves his hand and reaches for Suri. When he touches her upturned hand, she jolts. Her entire body trembles, and then her body softens considerably.

"What happened?" I demand, as protective fear pushes me to my barest limit.

"I-I don't know," Tyran says, but his voice is shaky enough for me to ask again. Korday cuts me off when he orders Tyran to leave. Tyran hisses aggressively, his heat heightened again, but he moves away without a fight.

A pinch on my right leg catches me by surprise, and I snarl in response. Then another one on my left arm, then my right arm until there are so many tranquilizer darts, I can't count. My head droops like I've lost control of its weight, my surroundings blurring and heavy. A verbal argument ensues, but all I hear is the canned sound of my own blood rushing through me until I no longer hear anything, and unconsciousness yanks me into its vulnerable hell.

Chapter 10: A Lamb to Slaughter (Kilian)

Two days.

It takes two exhausting days for the Gargoyles to torture me beyond my healing abilities. Without nourishment of fresh blood, the healing drains me of the strength needed to escape. At first, they beat me while I was drugged and unable to protect myself. My body automatically healed itself, not giving me the chance to reserve what I needed to survive more days without feeding. Then my arms had been strapped in silver shackles that burn when I yank too hard. The shackles are attached to silver chains connected to a thick silver bar that spans across the length of the small cell.

Closer to the silver door that blocks me from escape, a long shaft leads upwards to an opening the size of a Gargoyle. In the daytime, the sun obstructs any chance of escape. At night, though, the moon teases me to embrace it once more, to bask in the protective power of her darkness.

Weak and starving, I can barely hold myself up, jolted back to consciousness when my wrists touch the silver shackles. I heal while I'm asleep, but I can't sleep because my wrists will touch the silver and jolt me awake, anyway. I can't even let my body relax enough to breathe or rest.

There were times in my delirium when Suri's voice eased the pain. She quietly murmured her oath to Tyran, that she'd do everything in her power to keep me alive. As if a mortal held any power over a Gargoyle's strength and stubbornness. Still, her peaceful voice, full of caring and acceptance, resonates in my restless mind. Even Wrath stays away, making sure I live long enough to wreak its revenge.

Because the Demon will have its vengeance!

Suri's voice echoes from outside the cell door, and I smile despite the pain and feverish delirium. It gives me a reason to hold on longer until I find the chance to escape and strike back with force. The strong need to protect her is overwhelming.

The Risen Oath compels me to obey her, but I'm no longer offended by it. She'd suffered the painful pressure of the silver net over her body to shield me. After her ridiculous mistake in extending my life for her misunderstanding of the situation, I'd given her no reason to help me. Even so, she'd made demands from Gargoyles at the expense of her own reputation, one held by a thin thread for consorting with their enemy.

When Suri's voice grows louder, her demands coating each incomprehensible word. I crack my weary eyes open, just enough to stare at the silver door blocking me from reaching her. I groan quietly as the creak of its hinges fills the cell. It means more torture, and my starvation has already reached its exhausting limit.

I growl viciously and wildly thrash against the chains when the door is thrown open, more as an illusion of strength than a disregard to the agony of silver on my skin. Beyond the shaft of sunlight, instead of oversized Gargoyles bursting in to torture me, Suri's mud-brown eyes immediately meet mine, and unexplainable relief floods through me because she's unharmed. She *is* wearing a ridiculous Victorian dress that drapes around her like a curtain of too-much cloth, a matching corset that pushes her fleshy bosom up toward her lovely porcelain neck, making her look incredibly sexy and maddeningly tasty!

At least she's wearing gloves.

Tears swell in her eyes when she sees what's left of me. Even though she recoils from the smell of death and decay that surrounds me, she runs to me. Her body heat is a painful reminder of her warmth, her blood pumping so loudly in my ears that my gaze automatically falls to her neck, where the aorta artery pulses with sweet seduction. My fangs burn in my gums, and I can't hold them back.

Panic kicks me in the gut that I'm her greatest danger right now. I growl loudly, the sound more pronounced in the small chamber. Suri stops abruptly, slipping her lower lip into her mouth and gnawing at it. I groan with tightening desire.

"Stay away!" I snarl, my throat so parched the two words are like fencing swords. Suri stares for seconds, the quick sound of her breath and the loud thumping of her heart making it harder to concentrate on protecting her. Then she turns around angrily and berates the two Gargoyle guards. I grin, because that little spark of fire is as amusing as it's utterly confounding.

"I demand to see Korday," she's yelling. "Now!"

"He isn't here," one of the guards replies gruffly, but she isn't intimidated.

"Then find me someone else who will answer to this abuse! Not only does he kill my faithful cat, but now he's tortured Kilian despite his oath!"

133

The other Gargoyle scoffs with disgust and grumbles, "He's just a Vampire, an abomination!" Suri steps up to him, small despite her weight in comparison to the larger and wider Gargoyle. Wrath rips through my subconscious and my eyes narrow to dangerous slits. Not that I'm capable of doing anything to save her, but Wrath might be, even if it kills us all in the process.

"He's *my* Vampire!" Suri yells, undaunted by the bigger Gargoyle.

I'm as caught by surprise by her possessive declaration as the Gargoyle. My chest swells that she's acknowledged me as hers to a race of Supernaturals that despise Vampires as abominations, carriers of the virus that condemned Cain to expulsion from God's grace. Arrogant, sanctimonious sophists! My mouth twitches, and I'm not sure whether to scowl at being called someone's belonging or grin that I belong to Suri.

"Find Korday, or someone else who will answer for this! Now!" The guard stares at her, unsure of what to do, until the other guard sends him to find Zoji, another self-righteous prick, and Korday's mate. The Gargoyle runs out, leaving Suri and the guard with me.

"Get out while I speak to him," Suri orders the guard. She cuts him off when he tries to speak by pushing his arm like she can move him. When he doesn't move, she looks up at him, and scowls. It's so adorable I smile.

It has a different effect on the Gargoyle. He grumbles and steps out, and Suri slams the door closed, turns to face me again, tears instantly glistening her eyes. I panic, becoming very aware that we're alone, a mortal and a starved Vampire.

"You have to leave, Suri," I beckon weakly. "I'll kill you." She closes the space between us, grimacing at the smell of death the closer she comes. Her scent, though, only becomes more enticing.

"You are my Risen, Kilian Willingham, and I am your Mistress, Suriya Rovana. You cannot kill me. You *will* not kill me." The power of her words as Mistress ripples through me, rendering me weaker.

She makes a gagging sound and lets out a shaky breath when she adds, "But... But you may feed from me this one time." I growl, the offer too difficult to resist.

"I'll kill you."

"You will not," she replies with power and surety. Then she clumsily gets on her tiptoes, teetering twice before finding her balance. She wrinkles her nose and carefully wraps her arms around my neck, looks me in the eyes, hers such a bright amber they glow in the darkness that surrounds us. For the first time since I was drawn to those enchanting eyes, I bask in them.

Until she swallows hard, breaking my concentration and bringing my hungered gaze to her throat. That's all it takes to sink my teeth into her neck and draw first blood. Suri may have screamed, but I'm too lost in the bloodlust to have heard. I press deeper into her vein and the darker blood—her life essence—is sweeter than expected. It gushes into my mouth, filling every empty crevice, restoring shriveled organs, and reawakening my healing powers and strength.

She moans, but the sound pumps more madness to the need, and I suck hard on her throat, reveling in the life-giving power of her blood. Her body jolts, her fingers digging hard against my neck. The sharp pain mixed with blood awakens the Demon inside me. It yanks my arms from my bindings, and the chains clang to the floor. The silver shackles hang on my wrists with a tolerable burn that Wrath doesn't mind. I grab Suri by the waist and hold her up.

Satiated by her blood, I pull my fangs out of her neck with a satisfied growl, the last drops of blood coating the roof of my mouth with pulsating sweetness as it makes its final trail down my throat. My senses are sharper than they've ever been. Almost like the first time I'd consumed blood.

A cool breeze rides in the sunlight, gliding along my skin. I taste petrichor on my tongue, hear the coming storm and Suri's slow, weak heartbeat. Her warmth wraps my cold skin in an embrace I know I don't deserve. For the third time since she'd seen me, she's saved my life: once with her essence, then her body, and now her blood.

To Supernaturals, the number three is the magical link connecting the invisible cause-and-effect thread. Suri had called me hers and proved it three times. We are bound by blood and servitude, magic, and sacrifice.

I glance at Suri's collapsed form in my arms and gasp. Panic claws up my throat that I may have, in fact, killed her despite her confidence that I wouldn't. I quickly lick her wounds to heal them, ashamed that they're not just two fang-holes, but a gaping wound, like an animal had mauled her. If I want her to live—and I do! —I must get her out of here now, especially because I'm sure the Gargoyles would've heard the chains breaking.

I hold Suri by the waist, then slam one shackled wrist against the silver pole. It cracks open unceremoniously and its partner soon joins it on the cement floor. The door to the cells rattles with the heavy footsteps of Gargoyles coming. I peer up the shadowed shaft that leads to a partly cloudy sky. I can navigate the clouds, but my hesitation is for the sunny part of the forecast. The only way to survive such a flight without crumbling like burning paper while carrying a mortal is in a cloud of bats.

I've never spliced into bats, but I'd seen Tyran do it twice. He doesn't do it more often because holding one's consciousness when there are so many moving parts is more challenging than it's worth. Splicing myself while carrying an unconscious woman on the heavy side isn't exactly a good first try. But the Gargoyles are closing in. I refuse to remain a tortured prisoner, and Suri deserves my sacrifice.

The cell door bursts open and Zoji's dull gray eyes widen, then narrow in threat, her eyes blackening and horns poking through her blonde hair. I lift Suri in my arms, forcing myself not to notice her limp body and cold skin. Glancing into the shaft that'll take me to either freedom or death, my mind fractures into hundreds of parts, each with the same thought.

Escape.

My body splinters into a horde of black bats that shifts Suri between them with careful precision, carrying her up the shaft. I concentrate on holding the same thoughts in each bat, using echolocation to find the nearest cave or abandoned building. When sunlight brushes the first bat with warmth, my concentration wavers, and my forms nearly drop Suri. I refocus all the minds back into mine and burst into the gray day.

The bats undulate back and forth, holding the shape of my form in their movements while carrying Suri in their embrace. The clouded skies hold the sun at bay, keeping me from catching fire, and my concentration is absolute.

Along a wide river, a deep cave pings my interest and the cloud of bats follows my mental direction. The entire black column surges and swells with evasion and focus until hundreds of fluttering wings steer into the wide mouth of an abandoned mine. The cloud of bats carefully shuffles the unconscious woman, avoiding contact with rock and stone as the tunnel narrows, growing darker and colder until the tunnel opens into a cave.

Deep in the cave, away from Gargoyles and sunlight, the bats flutter in a circle around Suri, who is carefully placed on the rocky ground. In total focus, I visualize my legs touching ground, then mentally work my way up, ending with a final drag of my outstretched arms until all the bats are absorbed back into my body. I fall to one knee beside Suri, my chest heaving with exertion. My skin tingles, my muscles ache, and my fangs burn against my gums. The flight was as exhilarating as it was exhausting!

Instantly drawn to Suri, I glance at her pallid face and grab her hand. It's cold and flaccid. My chest tightens, panic meeting with hopelessness, an emotion I hadn't felt in so long I'd forgotten that it even existed. I pull her up to me and do something I haven't done since Annette died. I hug her. Though faint, Suri exhales a soft puff of air that loosens the tightness in my chest. I hold her tighter; not because I'm checking for life, but because I don't want her to die. But can a fugitive Vampire save the life I took during the daytime?

My head snaps to the left when the distinct scent of a supernatural reaches me, and I snarl my first warning, flipping Suri's body around, giving my back to the distinct sound of whooshing as a projectile narrowly misses us. I reach for a silver-tipped arrow and lift my head with a scowl.

"I don't come with ill intent," I snarl, the words gruff and hostile.

"The Hunter always comes with ill intent," a voice I don't recognize replies coldly. "Vampire assassin to both mortals and immortals."

"I'm not here for you," I sneer. A stocky man appears from the darker end of the cave, his dreaded hair long and gnarly, his blue-brown eyes unnaturally big and bright for his thin face, his whiskered beard barely able to conceal large incisors.

Werewolf. I hate Werewolves. They're aggressive, explosive, and reactive, and their musty smell always assaults my senses.

The man's bushy eyebrows rise skeptically, as if he can read my negative opinion of his race. From several long feet away, I'm aware that he holds a crossbow in his steady hand, another silver-tipped arrow pointed in my direction. While it won't kill me, it can hurt Suri and even kill her.

I glance down at her, held firmly in my arms, at a loss. I'm not used to caring for anyone but Tyran. The feeling is heavy and bloated, an uncomfortable warmth piercing me with unexpected longing for something else. Something more. My worry is not that I'll die if she dies. It's that if she dies, I'll not want to live. I turn to the Werewolf and sigh.

"She's dying and needs medical attention," I reveal in a low voice. He stares at me, his multicolored eyes bright even in the dark, definitely signaling him as a supernatural.

"Blood is life," the Werewolf replies coolly. "You should know that, Vampire." I frown, unsure of whether he's insulting me. But his expression is neither offensive nor judgmental. When the meaning of his words becomes clear, my stomach plummets and I shake my head, confusion and concern stocking the rapid-fire of my thoughts. Feeding my blood to Suri means Turning her.

Against her will.

Tyran and I vowed never to Turn a human, never Sire someone by force instead of invitation. Tyran had never forced my Turning. Instead, he'd coaxed me into it. Not necessarily full disclosure, but I wouldn't have cared even if I'd known the truth of his bloody eternal offer. Turning Suri without her knowledge would break my own vow even if it saves her life.

"Interesting," the Werewolf says quietly as he approaches slowly. "An assassin with a conscience. Or is that a heart? I thought Vampires lacked a heart. Or is that just a soul that they lack?" I clench my teeth, but don't show him my increasing annoyance. "Does the legendary Hunter lack a heart or a soul?"

"I'm not a legend," I grumble.

"Ah, but you are, Black Heart. Your reputation precedes you. Highly favored by the Vampire Courts, feared by the SupaCourt. In turn, you fear no one. Assassin of human and supernatural alike."

"Who are you?" I demand, more uncomfortable by his knowledge of me than mine of him.

"Tobias Winters," he replies freely with a mock bow. "Third and bastard son of Magnus Winters, Werewolf alpha of the Blackforest pack in the north."

I sneer with derision, "Why does an alpha's son hide in a cave with silver-tipped arrows?" The Werewolf must be on the run from his own pack, which will only bring me more trouble than he's worth. Tobias doesn't reply. He isn't even perturbed by my question. Or by me. I scowl warily, especially when his eyes drop to Suri. I instinctively press her to me, and he raises his brown-blue eyes to mine, understanding blooming in the large orbs.

"Your mate?" I barely conceal my surprise at his assumption.

Mate? Mates is a concept for shifters and lesser creatures. Vampires don't take mates. We choose life-long partners. Destiny and fate have nothing to do with companionship and mutual pleasure, especially when one partner can be replaced by another upon death.

"If she's your mate, then why the hesitation?" the Werewolf continues. "It's obvious she's worth the compassion of a ruthless killer. Perhaps the real question is whether she's worth loving for all of eternity."

Love? That's even more startling than his first assumption. Am I capable of loving a woman? Do I even know how to give love? Am I worthy of being loved? Could Suri love a Vampire Risen? The idea of being loved is one I'd never entertained, and that of loving is one I thought impossible. Women have come and gone over the centuries, but I've loved none. They simply served a purpose, whether human or supernatural. Tyran, on the other hand, wants only one woman who wants nothing to do with him. Is that his way of loving?

I glance at Suri's face and caress her cheek. Three days ago, I wanted her dead because I couldn't be the one to do it. Today, I'd kill to see her mesmer me with her bright amber eyes and order me around. She may not be my mate by race, but she could be my partner. She may be my Mistress, but I can be more than just her Risen. I groan and curse in Esperanto!

This is why I hate Werewolves and their emotions about everything!

Tobias's unnaturally big eyes catch mine, appropriately gauging my unbelief that Suri is my mate or that I love her, and he repeats with more solemnity, "Blood is life." My mind stumbles again on the concept of Turning Suri without her consent. But I'd rather Suri spend the rest of eternity hating me than spend the rest of eternity without her.

I lift my wrist to my mouth and bite. The cool blood flows freely, thick and slow, and I place my wrist over Suri's parted lips, allowing the drops to dribble into her mouth. The Esperanto vow I'd only heard once spill from my lips unbidden.

"I, Kilian Willingham of Victorian England, will forever rise by your side," I whisper as crimson colors her bluing lips. "I will guide you through the Turning and feed you of my own blood. I will stand between you and anything that dares harm you, shield you by day and hunt at your side by night." I pull my hand away, the wound immediately healing. Leaning my forehead to hers, I add my own words, even quieter than the Sire vows.

"I will forever be your love if you will eternally be my mate."

She doesn't move and barely breathes. She'll have to die to her mortality first, and Turning death is never peaceful. She'll convulse while my blood targets her immune system, killing her mortality, reviving her into immortality, and replacing her immune system with Vampire immunity. The whole process can take hours or days, depending on whether Suri survives the transformation.

I don't dwell on that last thought.

"I suppose this makes me your best man," Tobias interrupts, and I glare at him with irritation. He raises a bushy eyebrow. "You invaded my home and gave a Sire's vow to an unconscious human." He shrugs, turns, and walks further into the dark cave.

"She'll need a place to finish Turning, especially when she wakes weak and vulnerable."

"How do you know?" I demand with growing apprehension, his words tasting of threat. Something unsettles inside me, and the Demon raises its hackles. Interesting.

Tobias must sense it because he turns around and looks around suspiciously, sniffing, and searching for another supernatural. He'll never find it because it lives inside me.

Ignoring my question, Tobias glances at me and says, "You're welcome to stay here during the Turning." Unsure whether the Werewolf can be trusted, I rely on my knowledge that, even in my weakened state, I'm faster and stronger than any Werewolf. Wolf Shifters, though, are a different breed of fighters, but he's not a shifter. I pick up Suri in my arms and follow Tobias deeper into the darkness.

"You and your mate will leave my home when she reaches the bloodthirst stage," he continues. "I don't want to be a first meal, and you and I barely know each other to trust your word over your instinct."

I raise an eyebrow and reply, "I gave no word."

"Exactly my point," Tobias replies with a nod. He isn't upset about it, though. Only resigned.

As I follow a complete stranger into his home and hold the only woman I've ever wanted to spend the rest of eternity with, I graze my fingers over her cheek and whisper, "Survive this, Suri."

Chapter 11: The Werewolf (Suri)

Kilian leaned over the ship's railing, dry-heaving and miserable. He was no longer emaciated and cadaverous but full-bodied and healthy. His midriff was so tight it felt like his stomach gnawed on itself. Hunger daggered him mercilessly, stab after stab, until starvation became so complete it staved off the much-needed human blood, resulting in internal bleeding as his new body fed from his own blood!

Kilian had barely been able to hold off like most fledglings, despite his being unable—or perhaps unwilling—to take a life in exchange for his. He'd seen too much death in his life.

His mother.

His sister.

His father.

Kilian frowned deeply at the thought of him. He had killed the old man himself, beating him with his own cane. Father's absence had been the cause of both his mother and sister's deaths. He'd abandoned them when he needed them most, and Kilian had been too young to be the man of the house. When he did grow into the role, he beat his father to death and buried him under the stone fountain he'd commissioned days later in honor of his mother and sister.

Kilian dry-heaved again; not because he'd killed his father. That he didn't regret. But because he would have to kill other people for the rest of his existence. It was a price he would have to pay if he wanted to survive the Turning. Consumption was the last step to eternity and could only be reached by taking a life.

But there was something else that drove him. An evil and dark presence that had returned to life with him. Violence and anger throbbed beneath his skin. A living, breathing fury clawed at him with more resolve than the hunger. Ravenous for blood and death.

Kilian groaned in pain, rain pelting his exposed face and hair. It had been raging nonstop since he and Tyran had boarded the ship several nights earlier. Tyran claimed to have mastered atmokinesis and was controlling the storm that beat the ship mercilessly. Kilian was not sure he believed his declaration, but the coincidence kept the sun away and the humans huddled together.

Easy prey.

A voice broke through the rain and intermittent thunder.

"Mr. Hunter," the ship's quartermaster yelled his new name into the wind. "You and your partner must leave this ship immediately. You have brought death and disease onto the ship and are damned by God Himself."

He turned around and closed the space between them so quickly even Kilian was surprised. The quartermaster's eyes widened with fear as Kilian grabbed his biceps and brought him closer, his fledgling fangs burning as they broke through his raw gums. Despite the pounding rain and raging winds, he heard the quartermaster's heartbeat racing in his chest and saw the artery in his throat bulge.

Kilian's starvation turned vicious as it ripped through his stomach and skin, tearing at him with barely restrained violence. Kilian took a deep breath and stepped away without releasing the quartermaster. He wasn't sure if he could spend the rest of his existence taking the lives of others just to extend his own.

The sound of flintlock and burning pain in Kilian's side surprised him for a split second before rage, fury, and violence were unleashed with supernatural extremity.

The quartermaster's eyes bulged with fear. Kilian's flickered black and narrowed. He blinked, unaware of the fine line between light and darkness. When his eyes opened, his fangs were already ripping through the quartermaster's neck, tearing it like an animal. Kilian blinked, the temporary darkness disorienting and fearsome. When he opened his eyes again, he was at another man's neck, rupturing his artery with ruthless disregard to those who watched in horror, their frightened cries and screams echoing in his ears. He lifted his eyes for a second to find Tyran staring at him with shock and a hint of fear.

Kilian grinned with cynical smugness, smashing the victim's head against his kneecap before leaping on another terrified victim and resuming the feeding frenzy.

Darkness flashed for long seconds before Kilian noticed he was surrounded by dead bodies, blood mingling with rain like crimson oil in water. Tyran's eyes glowed red, the power of his Sireship buckling Kilian to his knees until he heaved the engorgement of blood and wept for the last time.

I wake with a sob caught in my throat, my head pounding so badly I can barely crack my eyes open. The coppery taste of blood fills my mouth, and I gag, but there's nothing there other than the remnants of a dream, an absorption of the experience of Kilian's first feeding.

My hand instantly goes to my neck where Kilian had bitten me and my eyes fly open, but darkness swallows me in pitch black. While the wound has healed, panic seizes me in my inability to see, my eyes blindly swiveling in my head, terrified that I may have lost my sight from Kilian's extreme feeding. There's only deep, dreadful darkness.

My mind darts back to the last days from being knocked out when trapped under the Gargoyle's net when I'd tried to protect Kilian from the burning effects of silver. I knew it was foolish, but it was the only thing I could do to avoid seeing my Risen hurt.

Then I'd awoken in the massive Gargoyle castle, made of stone slabs, concrete, and cement, and was treated like royalty. I was given a bath and strange clothing that belonged in the Victorian Era but made my assets look almost sexy, though I kept my gloves, and was well-fed. But at the expense of Kilian.

I'm treated this way because I'm a Ternion. If they hadn't known I have the gift of Psychometry before, they do now. I refused to touch everything, claiming to be afraid and unsure of the supernatural world, but Korday isn't stupid even though he respected my wishes that no one would come near me.

I kept asking about Kilian and was given the runaround about keeping me protected from the Vampire. I tried to explain that I'm more protected by him as my Risen than by strangers I barely know.

They didn't like my response. Every time Korday tried to explain that it had been the SupaCourt who'd requested the Gargoyle's help in finding me, I avoided the conversation and demanded to see Kilian. I had little faith in the SupaCourt. I'd assume that Kilian had been hired to assassinate me by whatever Vampire Court he'd taken me when he mesmerized me. It was very unlikely the SupaCourt didn't know.

When Korday was called to meet with the SupaCourt about my presence, I took advantage of the guards and demanded to see Kilian. When I finally went to see him, shock robbed me of my words. He was gaunt and gray, looking so much like his natural form, the smell of death and decay sweltering the cell. I forced myself not to cower and turned it into indignant anger and determination to do the right thing.

Kilian's feeding, though, had been brutal and swift. His fangs tore through my skin like stab wounds, digging deeper, ripping into muscles and tendons until it was too late, and I could no longer cry out in horrified pain. He tore through my neck and vocal cords like a wild animal, the Gargoyles unable to hear Kilian as he regained his strength through my blood. I trusted Kilian wouldn't kill me. Maybe I trusted the Risen Code too much because I hadn't considered the agony of his feeding. It was a welcoming reprieve when I lost consciousness from the loss of blood. And now I may be blind from it!

"You look more... robust than you did when your mate brought you in." The sound of a voice, a voice *not* Kilian's, startles a scream that echoes in the cavernous walls. My breathing stills while my chest tightens like a fist.

The man grunts and mutters dryly, "Please don't scream. Sensitive ears." I scurry away from the voice, my hands touching rock and dirt.

"Where's... Hunter?"

"Still high-pitched," the stranger complains disapprovingly, and I frown, my mind gathering clues in the blind. Rock, dirt, and an echo may indicate that I'm in a cave. It's cold and damp, and I reflexively rub my cold hands together, then inhale sharply. Where are my gloves?! If the man has sensitive ears, he may be a supernatural, which probably means he can see me just fine in the pitch darkness. I refuse to show my fear, even though I'm sure he can smell it.

I release my bottom lip, sit up straighter, and warn in a more tremulous voice than my demand, "Don't come near me and don't you dare touch me."

"Your mate will kill me if he smells my scent on you." The easy, matter-of-fact tone doesn't match the self-warning.

"He's not my mate," I argue pointlessly, but it's followed by a stretched silence that speaks of his doubt. "Who are you?"

"Tobias Winters at your service," he replies, the rumbling voice sounding much closer. I press my back against a rocky wall. "Your mate brought you to my home in a cloud of bats." My brain hiccups before I realize what he's just said.

"A cloud of bats," I repeat slowly, amazed Kilian has the power to do that. I would've loved to have seen him do it! I want to ask the stranger to describe the scene but am not sure whether he's lying for attention.

"He awoke earlier than you did and left to feed." I pull up my knees to my chest and wrap my arms around them, shivering in the cold darkness.

"Do you… know him?" I ask tentatively, hoping he's a friend I could trust. His response gives me no hope.

"Only by reputation," he admits. I highly doubt Kilian's reputation is favorable. "How are you feeling? Any headache or muscle aches? Pains?"

"Um…" I assess my body and determine that I'm just hungry. "Hungry?" The silence stretches and I frown, wondering whether Tobias is judging me in the darkness based on my weight. He must assume I'm just hungry because I'm overweight. He did call me robust.

"Are you hungry for blood?" he continues, surprising me.

"What? Why would I be hungry for blood? I'm not a Vampire!"

"Your mate is."

"Ugh! He's not my mate!"

"He *is* your Sire, though." His words crash into me, and I freeze, staring into a darkness that's shrinking by the minute.

I   inhale sharply and ask, "Did he have me ingest his blood?"

"He did," Tobias replies in that matter-of-fact way I'm beginning to hate. As if being Turned isn't life-changing enough, especially when it's forced against one's will. Even if I can't be Turned.

Ternions can't be Turned by any supernatural race. Nature was wise in ensuring all Ternions were human, avoiding tilting the balance of power between species. But for Kilian to have attempted to Turn me against my will is as despicable as a Vampire can get. Aside from painfully ripping my neck apart for his own survival, even if it was with my permission, he abuses my invitation by attempting to Turn me!

"Hunter knew you'd be upset," Tobias offers.

"Of course, I am!" I yell angrily, to which he replies dryly, "Sensitive ears." I stand, keeping my hands against the rock wall to gauge what I'm doing. The darkness is so complete it suffocates, claustrophobic no matter how high or wide the cavern sounds.

"Interesting," Tobias mutters, much closer than before. I yelp and try to lean further back, but there's nowhere to go. He's inches away from touching me and barraging his entire existence into my mind.

I already touched Tyran and foresaw the death of a woman he has strong feelings for. Not Kali. Another woman. Slim. Black, long hair. Catlike, green eyes, paler than his. That was a premonition to balance the psychometry done on Kilian. The balance of my gifts is only for the living. If Tobias touches me, it'll be Psychometry again, and I can't stand to be witness to another supernatural's memories and experiences.

"What's interesting?" I squeak.

"You don't look ill," he explains, undaunted by my trepidation. When I hear him move away, I expel the shaky and loud breath I'd been holding. Tobias tinkers with something metallic while my fingers lead my feet away from the noise. I have to get out of here, somehow! With or without Kilian!

I'm thrown off-balance when light flickers in the cavern and illuminates it. Blinking the darkness away, I shade my eyes with my forearm and then carefully lift my eyes to the biggest eyes I've ever seen on a grown man. In fact, they're segmental heterochromia, brown and blue.

He's hairy and disheveled, like a homeless man living under a bridge. But there's a sharpness in those eyes, *definitely* Supernatural, with a gleam of reflective light bouncing off them. They assess me and peruse me like he's searching for something along my body. He frowns, and I'm annoyed that he judges me based on my weight. I highly doubt the Victorian dress would have him frown with such disappointment. His predatory eyes meet mine, but they aren't his scariest feature. His Werewolf teeth fill his mouth despite the heavy beard. The large, thick canines dominate everything else on his face aside from his intelligent big eyes.

He lifts a dirty-blonde eyebrow and says amusedly, "You don't approve."

Embarrassed that I disapprove, I mumble, "I don't remember how I got here or why Hunter would leave me with a complete stranger."

"He made the Sire vow to feed you during your Turning," Tobias explains and leans his muscular frame against the rock-wall. He may be hiding beneath drabby clothes and excessive facial hair, but there's no question he's built to be fast and strong.

I stare, my brain rummaging through tomes and ancient scripts trying to remember the Vampire Sire Oath. But there're only tidbits of Esperanto words. Damn the complicated language! Something about rising with me. Or is it guiding me somewhere? Whatever it is, the last thing I want is to drink blood. What I really want is a bacon cheeseburger with fries and a large soda!

I jump when Tobias's laughter echoes in the cavern. His smile is friendly, almost contagious like he'd be the kind of guy I'd hang out with at a bar after work. If I hung out with people. Or ever went to a bar.

"Do you always speak your thoughts out loud?"

I frown and say indignantly, "No!" His smile widens like he doesn't believe me but isn't offended that I'm being wholeheartedly truthful.

"A bacon cheeseburger with fries and a large soda," he repeats, and my body flushes with embarrassed heat.

I roll my eyes, failing at hiding an equally amused smile, and concede, "Okay. Sometimes I do. So what?" He chuckles, the sound relieving some tension.

"Now I see why the assassin would choose you to mate with."

"He didn't choose me to mate," I clarify. "If anything, I chose him."

Tobias crosses his arms and says congenially, "Now I find it hard to believe that a human, no matter how cute, can want anything to do with a Vampire killer such as Hunter." I frown and find myself defending my Risen.

"There's more to him than just killing."

Tobias cocks his head with interest and agrees, "That is true, otherwise he wouldn't have been so reluctant to offer you his blood."

"What do you mean?" I say too quickly. Reluctant? He *didn't* want to Turn me?

As if reading my mind, Tobias confirms, "It seems your mate does have a conscience, though sorely limited." I frown. "He and I aren't friends, but he was conflicted when I suggested Turning you."

"Why the hell would you make such an invasive suggestion?" I declare with indignation.

He taps his ears suggestively and says, "Because a mate gives his life for the woman he loves." My eyes widen, and I know my mouth is slack, but I'm not sure whether to purposely raise my voice to his sensitive ears or laugh out loud until they bleed.

"You think he loves me?" I mutter, then exhale heavily and shake my head. "You have it wrong. Our relationship isn't like that."

"He seemed pretty conflicted," Tobias insists, pushing away from the wall. "He brought you in a cloud of bats and was visibly upset that you were dying."

"Not because he loves me," I clarify, crossing my arms. "Because he needs me." Tobias watches with his odd eyes that see too much. Know too much.

He shrugs and slowly walks toward me, saying, "He spoke the Sire's Oath, but added to it." He stops a foot from me with his matter-of-fact expression but doesn't explain. I lift my eyebrows with impatient curiosity, and he smirks. "It's not my place to tell you."

"Apparently, it's your place to tell me about it," I reply, and he chuckles.

"What is your name, fledgling?"

"I'm not a fledgling," I grumble, pushing away from the wall. "He can't Turn me." Tobias raises a bushy eyebrow with intelligent curiosity.

"The first stage of traumatic grief is denial," he suggests wryly, and I roll my eyes. "Then again, you don't show any signs of Metamorphosis, the second stage of Turning." Unlike the less-publicized documentation of a Sire's vow, the stages of Turning and their side effects are published both from Supernaturals and humans.

Tobias's big eyes suddenly meet mine, the space between us too close when he assesses, "I don't detect any dilated eyes or coughing. Are you suffering from chills, body aches, headaches, stomach cramps?"

I step away with a frown and mutter, "No. I am hungry, though." His eyes widen with mischief, so I quickly add, "Not for blood."

"For a bacon cheeseburger and fries with a large soda." He smiles. I sigh heavily, glance at the only exit from the cavern, and head towards it.

"There wouldn't be a fast-food restaurant outside this cave, would there?" I say, my stomach rumbling like a low-gear truck. "Because I really need to—" I screech as the next step I take only yields air instead of rock and I find myself plummeting through it.

Tobias breaks my fall, grumbling, "Sensitive ears, fledgling, even if a six-foot drop does justify a scream." His words fade when his palm touches mine, and his memories and emotions instantly flood through me.

Chapter 12: The Mating of Three (Suri)

The naked blonde-headed youth covered in blood breathed heavily. His body ached with agony, his jagged skin folding and curling from large scratch wounds. The worst of them was on his back, where the two Werewolves unexpectedly jumped him after the pack meeting. Anger had simmered too close to the surface at the meeting, but the two men couldn't act on their inner violence in the presence of the pack elders and their Alpha.

The Alpha had known, though, that the men would take the fifteen-year-old and either kill him for their position in the pack or beat him near death to keep him in his place to guarantee theirs. The Alpha simply wouldn't get involved, even if they were his sons, including Tobias.

Anger and indignation still warred inside the boy's heaving chest as he glared at the Werewolves drowning in puddles of blood. Though the boy's body was torn and gashed, these Werewolves were so ripped apart that their features were barely discernible except for bloodied patches of hair, one dark brown and the other tan, barely hanging on to elongated skulls. Large bloodied canine teeth lay at the boy's feet, surrounded by too much blood.

When their bodies began to change back to their human form, Tobias's anger turned inward, horror clawing his conscience for what he'd done. The identical forms of two men in their mid-twenties materialized. Though he'd known them his entire life, they were unrecognizable, their physical forms forever stuck in their violent aftermath of their last battle.

Tobias stared, horrified by what he'd done, guilt ripping through him that he felt vindicated at the same time. But what would the Alpha do when he finds his sons dead from an unsanctioned fight for dominance? Would he agree that the fight had been necessary and indicative of his position in the pack?

No. He wouldn't. Kragen would never see his sons as they had been when they'd left the pack meeting. Young. Virile. Powerful. Arrogant. Entitled.

None of his sons.

The boy turned away from the protective enclosure of Black Forest, the pack where he'd been raised. The one that by right if not by pureblood belonged to him. The one he would never return and never claim as his.

I exhale heavily, Tobias's first explosive memory, one of blood. Not like Kilian's memories, where ingested blood is coupled with extreme violence. But Tobias's memory is incomparable to the emotions that torment him. They're so overwhelmed by sorrow and grief that I physically bend over in pain, vomiting whatever blood Kilian had given me, sobbing for a younger Tobias who's carried these heavy emotions for too long. Alone.

An angry growl echoes in the cave, competing with my loud sobbing. It's followed by an even fiercer growl, one I recognize, as a cold breeze whooshes past me, nearly knocking me down. I turn to the unmistakable sound of cracking bones and fury. My eyes widen in fear as Tobias grows at least two more feet. His ribcage widens to an unnatural width. His thighs expand, his knees bending forward and his heel breaking backward. While he'd been frightening before with his oversized Werewolf teeth barely fitting in his mouth, they're larger, scarier, and bared in an elongated muzzle, curled in an angry sneer.

I scream in sheer terror at the sight.

Kilian swipes a clawed hand in his direction, the sound like sharpened knives ripping through flesh, slashing Tobias's bare chest and face. Tobias howls in pain, swiping his claws at Kilian but Kilian is too fast, and Tobias misses. With abnormal speed, Kilian grabs him by the neck and throws him against the furthest wall. The sound resonates in the cavern as Tobias's mutated form crumples to the ground. But he has no time to return the blow because Kilian is up in his face, his fingers wrapped tightly around his neck.

Tobias growls, brings up his powerful legs and kicks Kilian with so much force Kilian flies in my direction. Kilian flips his body around without hitting the ground and, for a split second, his eyes meet mine. They're not cunning silver or angry black.

They're Wrath red! Wrath smirks with evil glee and turns his attention back to Tobias. It's going to kill him!

I rush to grab Kilian's hand and drag Wrath's attention to face me, whispering fiercely, "Wrath!" I wrap my hands around Kilian's forearm, pressing my body flush against his. Wrath turns to me, forehead burrowed with vicious fury, eyes burning with rage. I shiver but place trembling hands on Kilian's cheeks. His brow furrows even further, his grimace revealing top *and* bottom fangs. My heart pounds hard because I've never seen a Vampire with two sets of fangs. My breath come in short puffs of fear, my nose flaring.

I'm frightfully aware that Supernaturals are only driven to more madness by the scent of fear, and I'm by no means a brave person. I've been hiding behind clothes and books to avoid humans and Supernaturals because it has kept me safe from being touched and used, abused and killed. But I can't hide now. Tobias's fate is

160

linked to mine, and I care too much about Kilian to watch a Demon use him.

I take a deep, shuddering breath and whisper, "I-I see you, Wrath, and accept you. I have no intention of banishing you. I…" I swallow hard at my next words. "I willingly bind myself to you for as long as Kilian is bound to me."

Wrath watches me, its angry expression smoothing into a cold, hard, and unyielding stare. It doesn't believe my declaration. Agitated by its non-response, I realize I need it to believe me, to witness my sacrifice to it and accept my libation of words to save my more-important Risen. I don't know if Nana can break Kilian's bond to me, much less know how to banish a Demon, so I need Wrath on my side. Or, at least, I need it to let Kilian willingly protect me if Nana breaks the bond.

Wrath's stare narrows at my silence, and I do the only thing I can think of to gain some leverage and prove that my word is my bond. I get on my tiptoes until I'm nose-to-nose with Kilian and press my lips to his.

Kilian doesn't move, and neither does Wrath, but Kilian's lips are cool to the touch, though softer than I expected. A thrill of excitement emboldens me, and I slowly run my tongue over the delicate smoothness. I've never kissed anyone before. The fear of Psychometry is a constant reminder that a kiss might not be the only thing I'd take with me. But I don't have to worry about Psychometry with Kilian.

He inhales sharply and Wrath exhales a smoky breath that doesn't feel threatening or violent. An unexpected rush of desire surprises me when they both kiss me back, Kilian with his lips and Wrath with the fangs. My entire body trembles at the feel of Kilian's frame as he leans over me, his hands firm on my wide hips. He pulls me flush against his hardness and dips his tongue into my mouth, claiming me and setting my body on fire.

The kiss is lingering. Seducing. Sensual. Hungry. Intense.

My knees weaken in Kilian's embrace, and I'm keenly aware of how addictively he invades all my senses. My heart pounds when his unretracted fangs graze my tongue, spearing me with excitement and fear. The sting startles and, unexpectedly, arouses me when his fang pricks my tongue. A hundred sensual voices echo around us when Wrath growls with desire.

For the first time in my life, I don't shy away. Don't push away. Don't deny myself a pleasure I thought I'd never come to appreciate. To be touched without fear, without misgivings, without regret. If anything, the warming of Kilian's tongue with mine and the hot breath of Wrath's lust, though jarring, are also inviting.

"Demon!" Tobias whispers, breaking the moment. I hold Wrath's attention from Tobias before it kills the Werewolf. Wrath watches me with narrowed, lust-filled eyes, grabs me by the neck and squeezes. Not roughly. But possessively.

"My mate," it announces in its sinister voices.

My heart races and I swallow hard at his threatening declaration, but murmur, "Yours." It yanks me toward it and slams its mouth against mine, splitting my lip, then sucking it. I moan because it's wild and painful, sensual and arousing. I nip at Kilian's tongue and Wrath releases my throat, returning Kilian to me.

Kilian groans when he sucks the coppery blood and deepens the kiss. By the time I'm aware of my own body, my hand has slipped under his shirt, chubby fingers meeting hard abs that radiate incredible heat for a Vampire. Kilian pulls up my loose sweater, exposing my girth and my self-consciousness. I try to hide myself, but his fingers reach up to my breast and my mind blanks while he gropes.

"Mine," It whispers in my ear, Kilian's hot tongue grazing my earlobe, reaching all the way down to my core where I pulsate for him.

"You vessel a Demon," Tobias informs coolly. I hold my breath, gauging Kilian's reaction, but his tongue laps at my neck and I bite back my moan, so Tobias doesn't hear it. From over Kilian's shoulder, Tobias carefully watches Kilian.

"Go," Kilian orders, without turning to face him. Tobias's body tenses, a rubber band ready to snap, ready for another fight. But he surprises me when he silently turns and stomps away without turning back.

Before I can speak, Kilian murmurs, "I fed from the sweetest, most powerful blood that gave me renewed strength, but it left you mangled." I shiver at the memory. He pulls me closer, the gesture as intimate as it is gentle. Unsatisfied, Wrath roughly grabs the back of my neck, slips Kilian's fingers to my hairline, and yanks back, emitting a painful groan.

"Now I will feed *you*," Kilian announces and sinks his fangs into my carotid, delivering the aphrodisiac toxin from a hollow in his fang straight into my bloodstream. My body bucks with desire, Kilian groans, and everything changes.

The cool breeze grazing along my naked thighs.

The warm caress of Kilian's tongue.

The sudden thrust of pain and pleasure.

An unforeseen fusion of hell, heaven, and earth.

Death, life, and something in between.

Something unexpected.

In the end, we tremble in each other's arms, a Ternion, a Vampire, and a Demon. When Kilian releases me, his silver eyes hold mine and I'm as captivated by them as he is by me.

He leans in and asks, "What just happened?" I exhale a nervous laugh, feeling boneless in his embrace. He holds me up and pulls me closer.

"I'm not sure," I answer honestly, because I don't know what it means to be mated to Kilian *and* Wrath or the details of what that looks like with two different entities at the same time. The Seven Deadly Demons are only anchored to one vice, their own. They cannot be destroyed or killed, only banished to seek another vessel. And that's what I intend to do. But in the meantime, a thousand questions assail me with fear and apprehension.

Will Wrath abuse me? Rape me? Hurt me to the edge of death without killing me? Or will it join Kilian in protecting me because Kilian is bound to me as a Risen until Nana reverses the binding? The prospects are slim that Wrath, the Demon of rage and fury, would defend me in the face of danger, except to unleash its rage and fury. It is more likely that Kilian will learn to hold it back, keep it in check, if only when it comes to me.

As if sensing my fear and apprehension despite our intimacy, Kilian leans his forehead on mine and whispers, "I will be your love, Suriya Rovana, if you will be my mate."

Tears well up in my eyes because his words are so unexpected and so timely. I throw my arms around his waist, holding this moment tight in our brief embrace. He closes the hug and leans his chin on my head. We stay this way for only seconds that speak more than whatever we could've said to one another with words. Especially because I'm not sure he knows that Wrath has already claimed me.

When Tobias returns, his big eyes are drawn in a frown and his thick arms crossed over his troubled chest. I'm sure his lips must be pressed thinly beneath his beard.

"Does he know he's possessed?" I'm taken aback by Tobias's question, and so is Kilian. Apparently, no one has either noticed Wrath before or didn't survive witnessing its existence in Kilian.

"You've seen it," Kilian says coolly.

Tobias frowns and declares, "Of course not! I'd be dead or dying." His blue gaze pierces me with interest and another expression I can't interpret. Fear? Respect? "She spoke to it."

Kilian grabs my wrist and flips me around to face him. Instead of acknowledgment or anger, there's genuine concern. He leans down, his lips barely touching my ear, and I shiver. I can sense his smug smile at my reaction without having to see it, but I am also acutely aware of Wrath's possessive sneer behind the smile.

"You've made a deal with a Demon you'll come to regret." His words are dispassionate, but they're not cold. I inhale in surprise

165

when he leans his forehead against mine and exhales slowly, a mingling scent of blood and smoke.

"I have become your Sire," he says in a remorseful exhale.

"You have not," I reply, gently touching his cheek. It's cold and dry. "Ternions don't Turn. The balance of power would be thwarted by one race over the others and chaos would ensue. So we are created immune to Turning." Kilian leans away, his silver eyes wide with shock and relief.

"Ternion!" Tobias declares. Kilian turns to him with irritation. I wonder if we're the most exciting thing that has happened to the Werewolf since he fled his pack fifty-six years ago.

Kilian and I both stare when Tobias recants, "The dead will rise from ternary hands that hold a Demon's heart; a Seer's touch is guide and transit to reveal the Alpha King."

His words echo in my mind, and I recall the first time he heard those words.

"The Seer spoke of an Alpha King and his queen," the boy's father spoke, his voice a rumbling like thunder, his words lightning settling in the boy's chest.

Though smaller and the youngest of the Blackforest Werewolf alpha's sons, the blonde-headed Tobias looked nothing like his father, except for the eyes. He was the exact replica of his mother, a formidable alpha female who was not the alpha's mate, leaving the runt a bastard.

"This leader will unite all the Werewolf packs into one Court and lead with an iron fist, a Seer at his right, and a Demon at his back."

"How?" The young Tobias spoke quietly, the two bigger and legitimate sons of Kragen, cackling maliciously at the boy's question.

"Don't be daft," the older one, Roderick, sneered. He had his father's dark hair but not his blue-brown eyes. Tobias was the only son with his father's big, penetrating blue-brown eyes. The other son, Baldric, was taller but less ruthless than his twin, and younger by two seconds that had robbed him of his primogeniture.

"Because a Seer will prepare the Alpha King for what's to come," Kragen replied calmly, disinterested in the way his sons interacted. He was a firm believer in survival of the fittest. If the runt could prove himself worthy of surviving his older, bigger brothers and fight for his place in the pack, his father would respect it. If not, he wasn't worthy of having been bred from an alpha and born from an alpha's womb.

"And a Demon would protect his place as an intimidator and executioner."

"Demons are dangerous creatures, loyal to no one," Baldric argued, his voice deeper but softer than Roderick's.

"Some Demons need a host to survive in this realm," Tobias murmured, and his father's eyes shone with pride.

"You really are daft," Roderick mocked, missing their father's expression. "You know nothing about Demons, runt!"

167

Tobias slowly shifted his adoring gaze from his father's bearded face, his eyes shining with the acceptance Tobias desperately yearned, to Roderick. Even though he and Baldric were eight years older than him, Tobias wasn't afraid of them. He may have lost every fight against them since he was four years old, but he was smarter than both combined.

He was learning from Treznor, the Blackforest pack's SupaCourt representative. Gwenna, the pack's historian, was teaching him languages and history, and his uncle Nolan, Kragen's Beta, was teaching him and his brothers self-defense. He also taught a female pup younger than Tobias, but he didn't really know her.

The smaller, younger boy stared at the eldest son, withholding any evidence of the burning disdain and bitterness he felt against him and Baldric. Tobias knew he was special because Treznor and Gwenna had told him, and Nolan hinted at it when he'd grumbled about runts always ending up as alphas.

"The dead will rise from ternary hands that hold a Demon's heart; a Seer's touch is guide and transit to reveal the Alpha King."

The quietly spoken words resounded in everyone's chests. Kragen stumbled out of his seat abruptly, knocking it down to the ground with a thud. Tobias jumped to his feet, startled.

"I'm going to kill you, you little bastard!" Roderick growled, advancing on the smaller child, who instantly took a fighting defense stance. But Baldric stared in disbelief along with their angry father, both with their fists pressed against their heaving chests, having felt the power of an alpha in the small boy's quiet voice.

I exhale heavily and fall into Kilian's arms.

"He touched you," he growls angrily.

"I almost fell," I try to explain, breathless. "He saved me."

"More saved your ego, and maybe from some scrapes and bruises," Tobias adds. Though his words are droll, his tone isn't.

"We Blink to Nana's," I announce.

"Who?"

"Nana is my grandmother. She knows how to sever your bond and set you free." Kilian frowns, his fangs slowly making their violent appearance. I'm confused by his reaction and frown. "Don't you want to be set free from being my Risen?"

Tobias shuffles away and says, "You're a Necromancer?"

"I prefer Animator," I say dryly.

"And a Blinker." I groan impatiently because I just want to leave and get this over with.

"Yes."

"What is your third gift?" he asks suspiciously. I blink and swallow hard because Psychometry is so rare and highly coveted, and Tobias has a lot to gain from having me. But his destiny is aligned to ours, whether we want it to be or not.

"Psychometry." His big eyes widen, making them look even more abnormal.

"You know of the prophecy." I nod, and he exhales heavily, the breath he's been holding since turning his back to the Blackforest pack for what is rightfully his to claim as Alpha.

"Pack your bags, Tobias," I inform him. "You're coming with us."

"What?" Kilian growls, his fangs in full view. His angry eyes are swallowed in black, and he flinches when I touch his cheek. Tobias ignores him and heads deeper into the cavern.

"If you're not careful, I might think you're jealous," I quip nervously.

"You're mine!" The possessive tone should scare me. It should fill me with intense fear that a Vampire possessed by a Demon that has also claimed me is obsessed with me as my Risen. But it doesn't. Somewhere between giving Kilian life, making a deal with Wrath, and giving them both all of me, I accepted my fate.

With courage no overweight, antisocial recluse should have, I dare ask the Vampire Black Heart, "Will you continue to protect a Necromancer Mistress when you're no longer my Risen?"

"Of course!" he declares without hesitating. Tears spring to my eyes and I vacuum my lower lip into my mouth.

He groans and admits, "That is the most distractingly delicious bad habit!" I release my lip and he exhales, his eyes intent on mine, the black fading into two silvery moons.

"Will you only protect me out of duty?"

"No." He leans his cheek into my palm, a tender expression on his face.

Impulsively, I dare to ask, "Are you capable of more than that?" He closes his eyes, but there's no furrowing of his brow or frowning or scowling. He opens his eyes and pierces me with their sharp truth.

"I am your love, and you are my mate. Let's go find Nana."

Chapter 13: The Severing of Bonds
(Kilian)

I don't remember my mother enough to recall her face or her hair, or the sound of her voice. She was there until she no longer was. Annette had been different. I was the only parent figure she knew, and I ensured I didn't miss a moment of her short life. She had a soft, round face, with gray eyes like mine but dark blonde hair like Mother instead of my dark hair, like Father. It was sadistic irony that I looked exactly like my father and a relief that I hadn't seen my reflection on any surface since my Turning.

Annette, however, was beautiful. Not soft-spoken by any means, no matter how angelic her appearance. She had the most unladylike shrill voice even the servants frowned upon, more so the governess who constantly harassed her about it. Her laughter was loud and snorty, the kind that made the governess flog her poor fingers. I hid my smile behind my fist so I wouldn't be disciplined for encouraging Annette's unladylike behavior, but I loved to hear her laughter. Towards the end, it was what I missed most.

By then, I was more familiar with her crying, soft sobs of misery and pain. Those weren't loud and didn't disturb the governess, who left her post soon after Annette became ill. I spent many nights holding Annette in my arms as she sobbed herself to sleep, getting some reprieve from the illness ravishing her and giving me time to grieve without her notice. The one time I fell asleep while she slept, she died cradled in my arms.

I hold a sobbing Suri in my arms, her shoulders bouncing uncontrollably, her hot tears dampening my shirt. She does not cry quietly like Annette. Each wracking sob rips from deep inside her, a piece of her soul yanked from its place in her heart. They stab me—memories assaulting me—and I blame the sliver of Suri's essence inside me that feels her pain with such poignant misery.

Even the Werewolf paces with unease.

Suri had Blinked us to the hottest pit in America, several yards away from a lonely cabin in the swamps of Louisiana, where she'd instantly burst out crying, screaming, "No! Please, no, God!" Then, between sobs that made it hard to understand her, she'd begged Tobias to remove her grandmother's remains from the cabin and bury them beside her mother's grave.

It's hard not to feel her hurt, especially when she begged me not to let her get near the corpse until it was buried. She pleaded like an addict begging to be taken far from temptation, and I don't understand why she's fighting her nature. The cool breeze whips through Suri's dark hair, and everything is wet. We are several yards away from a swamp cabin desperate for repairs. Four sides of planks of dull-colored wood hold a sunken roof with a dilapidated porch sitting on stilts over rippling green water. The only item out of place is a well-furnished rocking chair on the small veranda overlooking the swamp.

Tyran and I had stayed in New Orleans in the early nineteenth century for a couple of months. At the time, it was the wealthiest and third-largest city in America, with enough people to feast on. We met Kali at a masquerade ball where she fed from the rich as a high-end madam. The patrons had highly prized her since her bright red hair and porcelain skin stood out among the darker-skinned gentry.

Kali knew exactly what Tyran and I were and welcomed us to feed from her so long as she fed from us, and we'd protect her from the supernatural courts that disapproved of Succubae in their already-corrupt city. It was mutually pleasurable until Tyran became addicted to her, and I grew bored. He and I went our separate ways for several decades before we met again in Nob Hill, where we fed from railroad tycoons.

Tobias returns from burying Suri's grandmother, looking very different. I wouldn't recognize him if it weren't for his wet dog smell. He no longer looks like a wild man but is dressed in a Henley

173

shirt and jeans. He's not as bulky as I'd first surmised but is lean and lithe. He cut his hair and shaved his beard, his hair a darker brown and his brown-blue eyes more penetrating. It's uncanny!

Suri swallows when she notices him. Her swollen eyes, a muddy brown, glistening with tears. Her cheeks are ruddy, her round face blotchy, her lips downturned in a frown that's more sad than angry.

She repeatedly hiccups before saying, "Where did you bury her?"

"Several feet away from the water next to another plot." Suri's body spasms as she tries to hold back her sobs but loses the battle and cries out, her voice broken with grief.

"Mother," she mutters and buries her face in her hands, her shoulders rocking to the rhythm of her grief.

"Suri, why not animate your grandmother?"

She lifts her head and says in a cracked voice, "Balance, Kilian. *You* were animated. The balance needs to be maintained." She bursts into tears again and wraps her arms around my waist, trembling with sobs. I hug her because I don't know what else to do. Her explanation is clear, though. The next time she touches someone as a Necromancer, she will take a life, not give it.

"The balance is precious," Tobias says to no one in particular.

I gently push Suri away and say dryly, "If you must take a life, take Tobias's. He understands the balance." Tobias shoots daggers from his eyes and growls, his teeth growing awkwardly in his mouth. I smirk wickedly.

"The pull is so strong, though," she continues. "The yearning to Animate is so powerful it rips me inside. Even though Nana's corpse has been dead for eight days, I can feel her body begging for life, yanking at me." She weeps her sorrow though Tobias and I don't understand her struggle. I never learned enough about Necromancers to understand their gift since my only concern was to terminate them.

"What do we do now?" Tobias asks instead of making another weak attempt at fighting me. The first drops of rain begin to fall from the clouded sky. Suri wipes her face of raindrops and tears, blinking rapidly to hold back any more errant tears that want to help ease her grief. She sniffles a bit more before she turns to Tobias, her expression solemn in lieu of her temporary breakdown.

"Tobias, I need you to trust me," she says, not at all what Tobias and I expect to hear from her. I frown but refuse to accept that I'm jealous of Tobias. Werewolves are too far beneath me to be given such a response.

As much as I want to have the bond broken, there's also a sense of loss. I'm unsure if I'm in love with the Necromancer since I'm a Vampire and we don't love, but I'm certainly attached to her like I was attached to the cat. If I miss Aislynn, I'll undoubtedly miss Suri if she decides to leave. I'll always know where she is because of the Blood Bond, but I don't know what the future holds for us.

I'll force her to stay with me. Or seduce her. I prefer seduction, though forcing her can be challenging and become a seduction. I'd smile at my conclusion, but Suri continued addressing the thorn in my side.

"I know I'm part of your prophecy and am prepared to align my fate to yours. But you need to trust me and not intervene with what I'm about to do." Tobias's big eyes narrow with suspicion and concern until he smooths his brow and nods. She turns her eyes to me then, the bright amber of the Mistress, and I frown. She asked Tobias to trust her but will force me to do the same, which means I won't like her following words.

"I'm not sure if this will work, Kilian, but please know that somewhere between watching you get hurt from the silver netting and seeing you as a corpse hanging from silver chains, I fell in love." I stare, dumbfounded by her declaration and slightly chagrined that I was considering seducing her through force for the challenge.

"You deserve to be free," she continues. "From both me and Wrath." The darkness inside rises, and Suri grabs my cheeks. "Wrath, I humble myself and ask that you please trust me. Share your consciousness with Kilian so you can both hear me." I blink, but it's long and slow, and I'm temporarily disoriented. My head explodes in pain when my eyes reopen, and I growl.

I own you.

Many voices speak at once, each one piercing my mind until I can barely hold myself up. I lean heavily on Suri, who's speaking, but so are the voices drowning hers.

I will not be banished!

"No, you won't!" Suri's voice breaks through. It's strong with determination, an authoritative voice that controls me. "Kilian deserves to be free."

No!

I clench my jaws to avoid the scream lodged in my throat. I've been nearly burnt at the stake twice by overzealous Pilgrims before Tyran killed them with Vampire Ancient fury and violence. I've been staked enough times to lose count and almost died from a stake before Suri extended my life. I've been stabbed, shot, and even maimed. I've been buried alive and face-down four times, chained and thrown overboard twice, and even cryo-frozen by a mad scientist. Tyran, who can find me anywhere in the world as my Sire, wreaked vengeance on them all!

But I've never felt pain like this!

"Kilian." Suri's voice is soft and gentle, soothing to the agony in my head. "I order you not to stop what I'm about to do."

"No!" I sneer because she's going to put herself in danger.

"Don't intervene!" she yells at Tobias. "Wrath, I told you I wouldn't banish you, and I keep my word. I exchange my body as your vessel for Kilian's."

"No!" I scream at the same time Wrath snarls, "Yes," the voices sifting through my mind with claws and razors.

"Trust me," Suri orders. Her bright amber eyes hold mine, and I frown but want to whimper. I want to reject her order and pursue my plan of forcing a seduction rather than exchanging a Demon. Her lips are on mine before I can argue. Wrath's breath is hot and heavy in my mind, but it's silent. When she gently tugs at my lips and bites, Wrath and I groan, desire rippling through me in heat waves. My fangs descend, and, to my horror, Wrath spears her. But she moans with desire, and I deepen the kiss, my fangs grazing her tongue.

I want to carry Suri into the rundown shack, lift the absurd dress the Gargoyles gave her, and bury myself inside her again, even if it's on her dead grandmother's bed. But she pulls away too soon and grabs my cheeks again.

"I love you, Kilian," she whispers and smiles sadly. The pressure inside my chest threatens to push through my tear ducts, and I'm too ashamed to release them. Tyran has never been ashamed of crying for Kali and me, and I shouldn't be either. But my last tears had been for Annette, and I've never loved anyone since.

Until now.

"I see you, Wrath," she continues. "And request that you sever your bond to Kilian and accept you into my body." She offers me her palm, her eyes bright and commanding. "Give me your palm,

Kilian. I will take Wrath's essence from within you to maintain the balance. I offer myself to you, Wrath, for the taking."

Red wisps of smoke escape from her palm as mine reaches for it. I try to will my muscles to disobey and not put her in danger of the Demon, but my palm still reaches hers, and the wisps enter my hand.

A cacophony of screeching voices screams in my head as Wrath is banished until my voice joins theirs. The agony of his expulsion is incomparable even to the awareness of his multiple voices in my head. The sudden silence disorients me, and I fall to the ground. My eyes are squeezed shut, the pain and agony gone, leaving only an emptiness that leaves me empty. Someone grabs my forearm and helps me up, but I'm unsteady, my legs wobbly, and my head foggy.

"Get yourself together, mate, before It wakes instead of Suri," Tobias urges. I shake my head and lean on him for support. I hate every second of it, but I'd rather let him hold me up than fall flat on the muddy ground at his feet. "Steady."

I hiss at him and open my eyes, a torrent of wind and rain bashing us. I expected to see Suri collapse in the mud, but she hadn't moved from where she'd stood when she exorcized Wrath. Her eyes are open, staring blankly ahead without any expression or movement.

"She looks possessed," Tobias voices my thoughts. His eyes are wider—not afraid, but apprehensive. I aggressively turn to him, my fangs instantly ready to kill.

"How is her fate aligned with yours?" I growl, but the fury that usually burns from the inside out is gone. Wrath is gone, and there's only justifiable anger. Tobias is taken aback, his canines filling his mouth, and I brace myself to show this dog how Vampires are superior.

But they recede before I can rip his throat out, and he replies, "It was prophesied that an Alpha King among Werewolves would rise through a Seer and a Demon."

"What?" I declare in disbelief and disgust. "She sacrificed herself so *you* could become king of your wretched race!"

His face darkens, and he tilts his head with affront but replies coolly, "No, Vampire. She offered herself as a sacrifice so that *you* could be free. If you think for one moment that she didn't have this planned way before she met me, you are as blind to her love for you as you are blind to your love for her."

I stare dumbfounded, not because Tobias dared to blame me for Wrath having possessed Suri, but because of the emptiness I felt when she banished It floods me with proof of his words.

I do love her. This is not affection like my feeling for Aislynn, my kindred cat. It's deeper. Stronger. Like how I feel for Tyran, but more protective. More intense. More complete.

I turn to her again, and my chest tightens as she glares, her eyes no longer amber or mud brown. They're red orbs streaked with black, the pupil a small black dot that makes her look sickening. But I'm not afraid of her, no matter what possesses her.

"Suri," I mutter, placing my palms over her wet face. "You are my mate, and I love you." Wrath narrows Its eyes, Suri's top lip raised in an evil sneer. "Suri, you are my mate, and I love you. Whether Wrath shares your body or not, you are my mate, and I love you."

Then I address the Demon in the same way Suri had, no matter how much it revolts my stomach. "Wrath. I see you and accept you." The sneer twists into an evil smile that breaks across Suri's lips. It tears me that Wrath uses her to express Itself, but Suri faced Wrath when It was inside me—perhaps more frightening with fangs—and so will I if it means getting her back. Suri blinks rapidly, and Wrath materializes behind her in a mist of fog and fury. Tobias steps away, the smell of fear annoying me, and I frown.

"If you're going to be Alpha King with a Seer and Demon, you better learn to accept them both." His eyes, darker in the rain and incoming darkness of night, narrow then drop, and he nods. He may be a stinking Werewolf, but at least he isn't a stubborn one.

Suri's mouth opens, and she shakes her head, still blinking, then chastises loudly, in clipped words, "We're sharing, dammit! You won't take over my body. Sharing means caring. Now move, please."

I stare stupefied, a typical response of late, but grab her in a hug when her eyes meet mine, a beautiful chestnut brown I appreciate more than ever. She laughs and wraps her arms around my waist. I hold her, the short time we've known each other flashing through my mind until this moment when I recognize my mate and love her.

"I know," she giggles. "You told me several times already." I hadn't even realized I'd spoken, and I smile. Not sardonically or viciously or wickedly. But a genuine smile I've only shared with Tyran and maybe Kali.

I release her, and she says, "Wrath and I made an agreement that—"

"Another one," I say dryly, and she smiles.

"A better one. Even though I vessel It, I still control my body. It will have to trust me, and I will have to trust that It'll only come out to protect me. It was not happy but acceded when I threatened to banish It from my body."

"You are one stubbornly brave human," I tell her and kiss her lips before she can argue. She responds, her lips wet and her tongue soft. I want to deepen the kiss and make haste to the cabin by the swamp to show her how much I love her, but Tobias clears his throat.

Suri pulls away and regards Tobias, her expression pensive and solemn. He watches her with the same seriousness, their destined fate evident in their silent connection. I don't care what it is. I intend to force myself into it, whether Tobias likes it.

"Tobias, it's time to claim your pack." Tobias nods and then smiles widely, his strange eyes bright in the darkness, his canines too bloody big for his mouth. I pull Suri into my arms, placing my chin on her head, my love expanding progressively in my chest. Tobias places his hands on her shoulder, and she Blinks us to the Blackforest Mountains in the north.

The End

Dear Reader,

Thank you for reading Waking Up Dead. I enjoyed writing it because what had started the enemies-to-lovers paranormal romance was a completely different idea than what you read. It quickly became one of those stories that take on a life of its own, forcing me to listen to the characters and let them set the pace of the novel. Kilian and Suri's journey to break their bond was only strengthened when they learned to accept each other— Demon and all!

Keep in touch for updates on Tobias' story in Waking Up King and my other novels and Kindle Vellas. You can email me at kamastersonscribe@gmail.com. I'm also on Facebook (www.facebook.com/kamastersonscribe), TikTok (@kamasterson_author), and Instagram (ka_mastersonauthor). Thanks again!

Made in United States
North Haven, CT
06 January 2024

46819770R00104